THE GIRL WITH THE GERMAN PIANO

THE SEVEN MOONS

Editing:
Chantal Brissac and Désirée Brissac Pereira

Translation:
Lynne Reay Pereira

Ilustrations:
Silvia Reali

Cover:
Rose Oseki

Contact the author:
sergioluizpe@uol.com.br

ISBN–13   9781983845635
ISBN-10   1983845639

THE GIRL WITH THE GERMAN PIANO

THE SEVEN MOONS
Sergio Luiz Pereira

Translation

Lynne Reay Pereira

Illustrations

Silvia Reali

STORY I

THE SEVEN MOONS

For Désirée, Chantal, Palmyra,
Francisco and Luzia

Contents

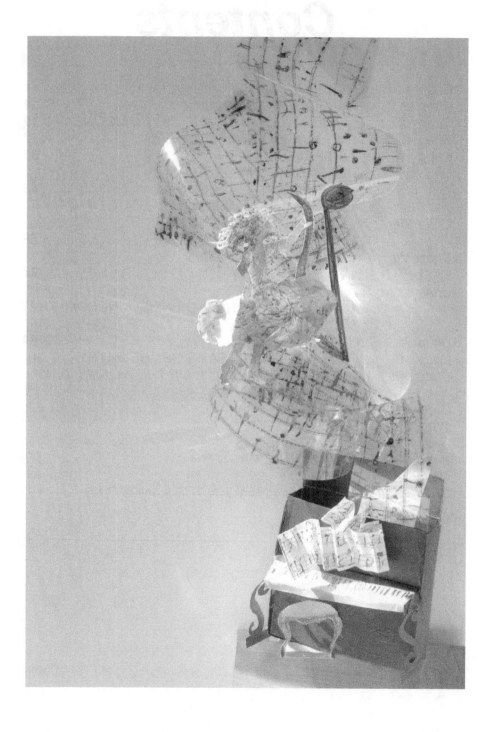

CHAPTER I

THE BEGINNING

They say that every story has a beginning and that everything starts somewhere. Stories almost always begin with "Once upon a time..." After all, men and women have always wanted to know the origin of the universe, the lives of others and their own. But does everything really have a beginning? One usually knows where and when the first encounter took place, that first instant when eyes met, the first kiss or the first quarrel. Is it possible to determine the embryo of love or hate between two beings? To mark with precision where and when the seed of an adventure, magic, spell or battle first sprouted? Would the seed not have sprouted if it hadn't been sown or planted in the soil? But when was the seed born?

Stories are like that: their true beginning gets lost in the mysteries of time gone by and we never know when or why they began.

And so with the beginning of our story. When that German piano had been built and through how many European hands, stages, houses and streets it had passed, no-one knew anymore. What is known is that it arrived in 1970 at the small house on Rua Independência, 1000 in the São Paulo neighbourhood of Cambuci, where a mother and daughter lived. The mother, famous for the flavour of her tomato sauces, was called Dona Carmela. She had been born in 1901, three years after her immigrant parents, Italians from the region of Calabria, landed in Brazil, never to return to their native land. It had been their daughter who used the best part of the severance pay she received after 28 years as a secretary in a pharmaceutical laboratory to buy that upright piano with the powerful sound, complex timbre, full of harmonics. It was a Bechstein. One of the best in the world when it had been built, tuners were unanimous about that. The design was classic and its colouring went from brown to mahogany, with engravings of flowers in beige tones stamped on the wood of the front panel, adornments that gave it a classical dignity.

When it arrived at Dona Carmela's house, the heroine of this story had yet to be born. Her father, Carmela's grandson and Antonia's nephew, was an adolescent and very distant in time, space and experience of life to know her mother, who had just turned twelve.

It would stay in that room for another twenty years. Then it would move, along with its owner, to a small flat. The old house where it had been, and the neighbouring ones, would be demolished by tractors and bulldozers insensitive to any romantic sentiment or historical preservation, emotions discarded by the insatiable financial hunger of progress that was shaping the city of São Paulo.

It would stay a further sixteen years at the new address, also in the Cambuci neighbourhood, until the moment it was given to the daughter of Antonia's nephew. Whether by chance or the force of unrevealed stories, the next residence – in another São Paulo neighbourhood, near Ibirapuera Park – would also be number 1000.

How many interwoven, interrupted, perpendicular, parallel or tangential stories did not involve that old piano? Facts that no one knows any longer. But the stories that it would come to experience with the girl would be many. So many, that not even half of them, whether through ignorance, lack of space, or even lack of time, are told in this book.

CHAPTER II

THE FIRST NOTES

Violet was seven when three strong, sweaty men came into the living room of the flat where she lived, carrying the piano, to deposit it beside the dining room table. Giving it pride of place in the room. She already knew Aunt Antonia's noble, heavy instrument; but, to this day she swears that at that moment it was love at first sight.

Violet began her lessons a year later. Her first teacher was a devotee of popular music and her initial training focused on this genre. She soon began to learn to read and play the first notes and tunes by the "Leila Fletcher" method. Her father, an amateur musician and proud owner of a fine soprano sax, often played duets with her. They performed simple versions of such pieces as Luiz Gonzaga's *Asa Branca*[1], Ludwig van Beethoven's "Ninth Symphony," and the theme music from Andrew Lloyd Webber's "Phantom of the Opera," itself an adaptation of a work by writer Gaston Louis Alfred Leroux, published in 1911. Violet loved that musical.

---

[1] Luiz Gonzaga (1912-1989), a Brazilian singer, songwriter, musician and poet and one of the most influential figures of Brazilian popular music in the twentieth century.

It was not unusual to see her imagining she was Christine, singing around the house like the main character.

Many people believe that magic has always existed in this world, and perhaps in the others, despite going unnoticed. And it was on a calm Saturday morning, when they played "The Phantom of the Opera" once again, that the magic in this story appeared. But we will never know if this was the real beginning of the enchantment that flowed subtly through the soul of the piano, which is its soundboard.

While Violet was playing, the instrument seemed to wake up and smile. Other sounds came out of it. Parts of these were not for common ears. They went beyond twenty-thousand hertz, the limit of human hearing, and also resonated deep, subsonic notes close to ten hertz. The audible parts were also impressive. It was as if Violet were in a concert hall, playing solo under the baton of an imposing maestro, accompanied by a grand orchestra. Her father noticed nothing. Incidentally, no one in that room, other than Violet, noticed anything. But everything passed very quickly for Violet, now eight years old.

The day took its course, running after the Sun, which was walking with Time in the blue sky of that cloudless morning. Her mother announced it was lunchtime and they went out to eat in a nearby restaurant. The city is full of living beings and, although they don't know or don't want to draw attention to it, humans are not in the majority in this population. Much less the supreme masters. The first in number are the viruses and bacteria. Then there's an almost invisible, though gigantic, population of insects. Following this in fewer numbers, though greater than the number of humans, are the rodents. There are also birds, cats, dogs and other creatures adopted and domesticated by us or adapted and living independently in the streets, on the roofs, in the parks, lands, holes, lakes and abandoned buildings.

The city does not belong only to humans, much as they would like to think it is. Angels and non-angels interfere within certain limits in the life of beings, whether in cities or not. And so the great link and the great magic created by God, which unite the life of everything and everyone, proceed in the construction of eternity.

As our five senses are fairly limited and the mysteries between Heaven and Earth are unknown, most humans follow their story with the main objective of "succeeding in life". Where succeeding nearly always means wealth, power and fame.

However, no person is without intuition and other senses. These are just dulled. On this day, Violet was feeling different. She'd heard what she couldn't understand and couldn't understand what she'd heard.

The night of a full moon and few – though twinkling – stars brought clouds racing in the dark sky. They seemed to be engaged in a dispute that ran towards the west of Brazil without any of them knowing where and when they wanted to arrive. Violet's mother looked through the window, sighed a delicious sigh, then closed it. She put Violet to bed, prayed with her and gave her daughter a lingering kiss on the cheek. Her father came to kiss her goodnight soon afterwards. This sequence was a nightly routine. She would snuggle under the covers and listen to a story told by her mother about a bird called Marie. Sometimes the stories would come from her father's mouth. But with or without stories, her father always made her laugh when he said:

"Remember, it's not the girl who hugs the bedcover, but the bedcover that hugs the girl."

And then she would fall asleep.

That night was no different. But at around one in the morning, Violet felt a touch. A slight tug on her ear. She opened her eyes a little. Her bedroom, like almost all the others in the city, wasn't completely dark: light bulbs in buildings and houses around stayed lit, evoking the insomniac side of São Paulo. The light from the streets, which doesn't stay alone there and rises to the sky with the smoke from human machines, also illuminated the early hours.

And there it was, poking Violet's face. Violet couldn't believe her eyes: it was a quaver. And like all quavers, it was quick and brief in its way of speaking. Much, but much briefer than semibreves. Its speech lasted four times less and it didn't beat about the bush

"Wake up!!!! Wake up!!!!! Let's go!!!!!! Hey, you!!!!!!!!!!"

"Ah!" This was the whispering sound that emerged from the back of Violet's throat.

"Wake up!!!! Wake up!!!!! Let's go!!!!!! Hey, you!!!!!!!!!!"
Now there was another light arriving in her room, a luminous light that twisted itself into the shape of a carpet that curved around the door .

"Wake up!!!! Wake up!!!!! Let's go!!!!!! Hey, you!!!!!!!!!! We don't have much time!!!!!!!!!!"

"Time? Time for what? Who are you?"

"Your friend!!!!!!!!!!! Your friend!!!!!!!!!!!!!!! Let's go!!!!!!!!!!!!!!"

"Where to? I'm scared."

"Don't be scared!!!!!!!!!!! Don't worry!!!!!!!!!!!!!!!!"

The quaver stood about 16 centimetres tall. It had the typical shape of a quaver, but with a face in the round part. This face had two eyes, a nose, a mouth and an expression. Which all faces have, whether they're human or animal. It moved around by hopping, because quavers only have one leg. At least in this detail it was a normal note. But none of this, which would have shocked any adult, attracted Violet's attention.

The quaver hopped onto the carpet of light. Violet understood that she was supposed to follow it. She didn't hesitate. The carpet proceeded to the piano room, leaving a bridge of light in its wake, and moved towards the piano. The lid opened. Sounds spilled out. They weren't typical piano sounds, but were rather the sounds of tubular bells. The volume increased and the rhythm quickened, along with the beating of the little girl's heart. But the quaver didn't miss a beat.

Dom!!! Blem!!! Dim dom!!! Blem, Blom, Blem blemdim dim dijmkiij djiii Chrzazzz!!!!!!!!!!!!!

And nothing more was heard. Violet had disappeared. The room, the flat and the city went back to normal. Only the little dog in the flat next door had noticed something different and wouldn't stop barking.

"Quiet, Chocolate!"

It was the shout from her owner that shut her up.

CHAPTER III

IN THE KINGDOM OF THE SEVEN MOONS

Violet didn't fall asleep, much less wake up. She just found herself in another place. The most distant place of her life. Now she and the quaver were the same size. They looked at one another, sized each other up. Who had grown and who had shrunk didn't matter. The field where they were standing was crossed by a dirt road coming from who knows where and heading towards the hills on the way to the high mountains. When Violet looked to the east, she could see a prairie then a vast river, clear and winding. Turning her neck to the west, she could make out a dense forest of very old trees. It looked like a great expanse of dark green blotting paper, into which the light of the Sun plummeted, never to come out again.

"Let's go now," said the quaver in the key of A.

As the quaver hopped away, Violet followed. It was just at this moment that the human noticed that everything seemed bigger. Bigger to the point of being at least twice the size that she was used to things being. The daisies and wild flowers couldn't fit in her little girl's hand. The bushes were very high and the trees – don't even mention them.

They followed the road that curved to the east, as if it wanted to quench the thirst that all that long dusty dirt road retained on a sunny day. When they were getting close to the last bend, before the road got to the river, Violet felt a sudden desire to throw herself into the water. The quaver had no time for anything. The little girl jumped in to the river in a zigzag of waters so clear they were actually blue.

Her elephant-and-lion-patterned pyjamas were soaked at once. Who cared? She was happy. She'd always loved the water. She'd learned to dive with a snorkel and mask with her father when she was six, in the seas around Ilhabela, an island off the north coast of São Paulo. And in her spontaneity, there was no river that could intimidate her. Near the bank, the tiny fish easily touched the river bed. A little further off, the river deepened with its river mysteries. The minnows fled from the little girl, who was given a good telling off by the quaver.

"What's this??????????????? What do you think you're doing!!!!!!!!!!!!!! Get out of there!!!!!!!!!!!!!!!!"

"Maybe notes don't know how to swim. Maybe they don't like cold water" she thought, enjoying every single second of that phenomenal dive.

As the note continued to fidget on top of the bank, Violet had no option but to obey and get out with her curly hair dripping down her face.

"Just look at you!!!!!!!!!!!!!!! You'll get ill!!!!!!!!!!!!!!"

"It's true. Notes don't like water. They're boring. They're kill-joys," she decided to herself.

"Get those pyjamas off straight away!!!!!!!!!!!!!!! You'll catch cold!!!!!!!!!!!!!"

"Take off my pyjamas and wear what?

"Ahhhhhhhhhhhhhhh!!!!!!!!!!! Now, see what you've done?!!!!!!!! I'll have to use up one of my magic spells!!!!!!!!!!!!!"

The pyjamas lay in a heap on the grass. Violet and the quaver didn't notice that this bothered an armadillo a lot. The clothes, covered in figures the animal didn't recognise, had become a wet, crumpled mountain in its path. The armadillo grumbled, looking for a new route. But who gives the least thought to the grumblings of an armadillo?

"And now?" asked Violet.

The note raised its leg. Between the staff and the leg, very well hidden and disguised, was a tiny chain holding three even smaller tuning forks.

The quaver shook its leg and one of the forks came loose, hitting the ground. The sound it made was a C, instead of A, as in tuning forks on Earth.

Violet saw nothing wrong in this because she didn't know that the tuning forks of human earthlings are tuned to 440 hertz or vibrations a second. She didn't know either that this, in western music on Earth, corresponds to A in the centre of the piano keyboard.

Although the tuning fork was very small, it had a powerful sound. Concentrating hard, the quaver made its wish. The trees responded at once, shedding many leaves. Close by, hidden among the flowers and the forest, silk worms in their cocoons woke up. Lots of butterflies came to help. Violet was encircled by those small flying beings, which wove new clothes for her in real time. It was exactly the dress that Joaquina the quaver had imagined.

Yes, Joaquina was the note's name. Since she had been born in a score of Renaissance music, she knew and liked the clothing style of her period. That's how Violet was dressed: like a princess or a girl from a castle. Violet didn't know that the fabric was special due to its magical weaving, It almost never got dirty. If some grease, stain or soil stuck to it, in no time at all its self-cleaning fibres left it looking as if it had just come out of the washing machine. It also shed creases and breathed in or blocked out the heat or cold according to the room temperature. But it wasn't waterproof. Though it did dry faster than our clothes do, without needing to go to the clothes horse or the dryer. On Earth, it would be called cutting-edge smart fabric by men of science. In that kingdom, it was just the raw material for clothes that never wear out.

Violet also got a pair of pink ballet slippers. They were beautiful, and fit for a little princess. It was just then that she noticed she was barefoot on that incredible journey, though she hadn't felt any chills on her feet.

"How lovely. I've always dreamt about being dressed like this." She did a twirl while watching the butterflies, silkworms and leaves going away.

"That's all well and good!!!!!!! But I used up a magic spell!!!!!!!!!!!!!!! Now I only have two left!!!!!!!!!!!!!!! Let's go!!!!!!!!!!!

No naughtiness!!!!!!!!!!!!!!!!!!!!!! Oooh!!! How pretty you look!!!!!!!!!!! Come on!!!!!!!! Good thing a magic freebie arrived!!!!!!

"Magic freebie?"

"Yes!!!!! The slippers, my friend!!!!!!!!!!! They came as a freebie!!!!!!!!! Good, good!!!!!!!!! Good!!!! Tchiboom!!! Good!!!!!!!!!!!!!!!!! Ta da!!!!!!!!!! Magic freebie!!!!!!!!!!!

The two of them followed the road skipping like two old friends. They were soon a long way from the river, where the forest spilled onto the road. Strong, deeply embedded roots wrinkled the surface.

"Oh my! So many bumps. They're good for tripping and twisting your ankle," Violet said to herself.

Joaquina suddenly came to a halt. She'd noticed a different vibration that was growing constantly in intensity and complexity of timbres. Like Ravel's "Bolero". But the music that vibration brought wasn't sublime like the famous bolero. Very much to the contrary. It was dark and scary.

It reached the brain through the ears and the bones of the body. As a consequence, the system of the three articulated bones formed by the hammer, anvil and stirrup of the middle ear, was being hindered in transmitting the vibrations generated in the tympanic membrane to the inner ear. And with this, besides the distortion, the music was becoming impossible to be memorized or understood. It was always feared like visions in the dark.

"Quick!!!!!!!!!!!!!!!!!!" was all that Violet heard as she was pushed sideways by Joaquina. The two rolled off the road, ending up in the middle of a thorn bush.

"Ouch!"

The quaver clamped the girl's mouth, stifling the sound the moment it came out.

"Quiet!!!!!!!!!!!!!!!!!"

"That hurts!" Violet tried once more, doing everything possible to get comfortable between the spiked, inhospitable thorns.

"Quiet!!!!!!!!!!!! Watch out!!!!!!!!!!!!!! It's them!!!!!!!!!!!!!!!!

The ground shook. Steps and dragging feet made everything shake. The atmosphere became heavy. The clear of day diminished because the light was blocked in part by the rising dust and perfidious vapours smelling like rotten eggs or a stagnant swamp. Violet plucked up the courage to take a peek through the thorn bush. She could make out a host of minims, quavers, demisemiquavers and hemidemisemiquavers all chained together. They were being pulled by a kind of steam-powered pianola, a bizarre instrument. Huge, rough and heavy, it had three main parts: a body and pianola keyboard, four wheels of brushed steel and wood and a steaming cauldron.

Heat radiated from a furnace that seemed to devour the wood thrown into it and also from a burner connected by a hose to a rusty domestic gas bottle. The pianola wore an expression of zero pity or compassion for the enchained notes. Inside it, the energy materialized by fire in the wood and gas passed in part to water, which turned into steam. It seemed efficient and effective. Effective, it certainly was; efficient, not at all. Just a tiny fraction of all that energy contained in the wood, gas and steam was turned into kinetic energy, as the scientists say, or into wheel movement. It was a total waste of energy. Even so, the pianola had enough power to drag those 82 unfortunate prisoners along.

Working as guards, another 20 notes patrolled the chained ones, pushing, insulting, mocking those that, through despair or exhaustion, couldn't manage to go any further.

Violet wanted to cry from fear and pity. She pouted. Her face crumpled. But Joaquina's stern look radiated confidence, which stopped Violet in her tracks.

How long did it go on? For Violet, Joaquina and the prisoners, an eternity. For the piano and the others, not so long. After all, they were enjoying themselves at the expense of the suffering of others.

Violet and Joaquina left the thorn bush carefully so as not to be pricked even more.

"Oh, this makes me so mad!!!!!!!!!!!!!!"

"It's very sad. It's not right."

"We have to hurry up!!!!!!!!!!!!!"

"Why do they do that? It's not right."

"Quick!!!!!!!!!!! Let's go!!!!!!!!!!!!!! The war's coming!!!!!!!!!!

"Why do they do that?"

"Let's go, Violet!!!!!!!!!!!!!!! We don't have much time!!!!!!!!!

"It's so sad...

"Are you going to start crying now????????????"

"Why do they do that? It's not right"

"Stop the pouting!!!!!!!!! Pulling that face won't solve anything!!!!!!!!!!!!!!"

Violet wondered what 'pulling that face' could mean and then followed Joaquina for more than a kilometre until they reached an uneven stretch of the valley.

"We'll go this way!!!!!!!!!!!!"

"But there's no road."

"But this is the way!!!!!!!!!!! It's firmer!!!!!!!!!!!! I mean!!!!!!! Safer!!!!!!!!!!!!

They went into the forest where the tall trees looked like old giants. Violet felt she was being watched. She thought the trees had an angry expression that followed every step she and Joaquina took.

"I wonder if they can walk," she thought, lowering her head to avoid looking at them.

"Even the trees are sad and angry!!!!!!!!!!!!!!!!!!"

"What do you mean, sad and angry?"asked Violet, not knowing exactly what world she was in.

Joaquina didn't reply. She thought it would be too much work explaining to a child from Earth that trees made their own music and that, therefore, they didn't agree with a music dictatorship that would hinder their eternal dance swaying with the winds.

Night soon fell. Between the tree tops there appeared rays of red, orange, yellow, silver, green, blue and violet lights. They broke through the wall of leaves and were at the same time absorbed by them. Some even reached Violet's and Joaquina's eyes and lit up the trail.

"How lovely!" Violet exclaimed.

"They come from the Moons!!!!!!!!!!!!!!!!!!"

Flying above the forest, an owl cut silently through the air, while in the firmament the seven Moons made point and counterpoint between the waxing, waning, new and full moon phases, performing a heavenly symphony not yet heard or imagined in the world of men.

CHAPTER IV

THE DANCE OF THE FLOWERS

This was the first time that Violet had ever been away from home, far from her parents. She would forget many details about this first great adventure. But the main part of this experience would always be in her DNA.

In the Kingdom of the Seven Moons – as it was called in that world – the flowers were also different from those on Earth. The night jasmine had the same perfume as ours and swayed in the wind with their lofty stems. They danced and exhaled a style of music that in our world was named Viennese Waltzes. Without becoming detached from their stems, they made little circles, as if they were dancing in the old ballrooms of Austria and Germany.

The roses were haughtier, and stayed where they were, simply exhaling their perfumes. The violets, more festive and smilier than the night jasmine, kept flirting with the carnations and provoking the anger of the roses and the envy of the daisies. The flowers shone when they received the rays of the Seventh Moon. And they had more intensity when this moon was full.

Each one of that world's Moons, called First, Second, Third, Fourth, Fifth, Sixth and Seventh Moon, was shining with its own colour. Like any particle in the universes, each moon had diverse reasons for existing. One of them was to protect the flowers. As their phases alternated in the Sky, there was always a different species of flower shining brightest at night in that natural ballroom.

And it was far from being just any ballroom, because the music appeared sometimes from the flowers themselves, sometimes from the wind blowing through the leaves on the trees. And the leaves, because of their different sizes, were like the reeds in such wind instruments as oboes, saxophones, bassoons or clarinets. They played with clear timbres and rich semi-low, medium and high tones. The thick trunks worked in that orchestra like tubas and the chords of double basses, while the slim branches and stems sounded like the chords of the piano and the viola. No orchestra in our world could or will ever have so many instruments. Impossible for any musical formation to be as rich, complex, broad and tuned as that one.

The Seven Moons were the main source of the melodies there. Each moon was also the patron and protector of an independent note in the octave being played at any given moment. As there were seven of them, they were the patrons of the musical structure based on diverse types and styles of scales of seven musical notes, which in the world on Earth had been initiated by the ancient Greeks and functions until today as a base for western music. The Seven Moons were the origin of everything related to the music of that and many other kingdoms.

Violet was enchanted. She recognized some of the music and questioned how that was possible. She asked who had taught the flowers, who was playing. She learned from Joaquina that the musical genre of duple metre, sometimes written in triple metre, which in the German language is called "walzer" (waltz in English), was much, much older than everyone supposed it was. In the kingdom of the Seven Moons they had already forgotten who had created it. Some claimed that the genre had been born with the night jasmine, the flowers that most liked the waltz, especially Viennese.

Violet also learned from Joaquina that, in the middle of the 18th century of human history on Earth, such great music maestros as Josef and Johann Strauss visited the kingdom of the Seven Moons in a dream while they were sleeping. In later times, other great masters like Frédéric Chopin, Johannes Brahms, Maurice Ravel and Johann Strauss II did the same.

"They did!!!!!!!!!!!! They're the parents and uncles of the waltz on your little planet!!!!!!!!! Little planet!!!!!!!!!! It's just a little planet!!!!!!!!!!!! If it carries on the way it is!!!!!!!! You'll end up with no little planet!!!!!!!!

"So, you mean...so you mean it was born here ?" Her little girl's eyes shone while she asked the question.

At that moment, the flowers and, especially the violets, the origin of her own name, noticed the girl for the first time. They gave an artistic bow. Then, they smiled wryly and danced even more gracefully.

Joaquina explained the principle of the inspiring muses and also told her that at times some composer is taken while sleeping to see concerts, recitals, shows or almost indescribable wonders like that in any one of the kingdoms of music. When everything was going really well, the art they watched ended up materializing more or less faithful to its origins in masterworks in the worlds of the composers who travelled in spirit during their dreams.

But Violet heard nothing of what the over-didactic Joaquina was saying. She was enchanted by the flowers. If she could have, she would have transformed herself at that very moment to become and be like them: perfumed, fresh, and in the arms of divine music. She'd be a flower bud opening up to life.

Everything was flowing well in that flora orchestra with no flesh and bone conductor. The fireflies, nocturnal insects, joined in the dance with their sparks of light functioning as tiny spotlights. They seemed to be competing with the rays of light from the Seven Moons.

Butterflies, not usually creatures of the night, bohemians or lovers of nightlife, appeared out of nowhere, joining in the dance the moment a great floral shindig began, with the flowers coming loose from their roots. Actually, a more appropriate term would be "a great stem-dig". The dance became more colourful when the lilies, including calla lilies, coming from the centre and spreading to the sides of the ballroom, began a step dance, or rather "stem dance," in the Irish style. Then they all joined in with New

Orleans jazz. The volume woke the bees and ladybirds up. Even those that couldn't fly, like caterpillars and centipedes, woke up. And, pollinators or not, they were all happy. Some wanted to dance flamenco while the dragonflies flew in the style of belly-dancing. The musical frenzy seemed to reach its peak. And the curious thing is that no one music style was in conflict with another. When they appeared in succession they did so in a surprisingly harmonic way. When they co-existed in time and space, though, they granted the listener the democratic right to decide which melody to appreciate. The only rule was that everyone had to be really good and motivate, each in their own way, the desire of any fortunate spectator to evolve. To be better. This was the main reason for their existence. They also wished for the health of spirit of anyone listening to them. And in this way, they helped to cure anything: lingering sadness of the soul, sick jealousies of the heart, despondency that also attacks the liver or any other illness of the mind or body.

The great forest stem-dig was very lively indeed and its reflections transcended that kingdom, inspiring populations from several other worlds, without their even being aware of what happened there every night.

Meanwhile, the roses continued to snub everything, assuming airs of being more important than they were. After all, as a great popular musician, the 20th-century composer and guitarist Angenor de Oliveira, better known as Cartola, once sang:

"Beat once more
With hope, my heart
For the summer is about to depart
At last

I return to the garden
Certain that I will cry
For well know I
that you don't want to come back
To me

I complain to the roses
But what nonsense
Roses don't speak
Roses simply exhale
The perfume they stole from you, ai

You should come
To see my sad eyes
Or, who knows, you used to dream my dreams
In the end"

"Bate outra vez
Com esperanças o meu coração
Pois já vai terminando o verão,
Enfim
Volto ao jardim
Com a certeza que devo chorar
Pois bem sei que não queres voltar
Para mim
Queixo-me às rosas,
Mas que bobagem
As rosas não falam
Simplesmente as rosas exalam
O perfume que roubam de ti, ai

Devias vir
Para ver os meus olhos tristonhos
E, quem sabe, sonhavas meus sonhos
Por fim"

It would be pointless to complain about or to the roses. After all, what nonsense. Roses don't talk. But if they did? What wouldn't they say about themselves or the lovers wooed and won thanks to them.

That was when the music performed by enchantment decreased in volume until it vanished, so that another could assume sovereignty. As sovereign as a haughty, yet friendly queen and her daughter, the princess, entering a chic salon for the Royal Ball. It was nothing less than "The Waltz of the Flowers". That lovely piece from "The Nutcracker Suite" ballet, performed for the first time to men and women of Earth on December 18, 1892, in the Russian city of Saint Petersburg, thanks to the genius of composer Piotr Ilitch Tchaikovsky.

Not even the roses could resist. All their loftiness disappeared: they simply joined in the dance.

What do humans know and when did they find out about the universes? How many vocabularies are there in the richest languages? Not even with all the science and technology mastered throughout the 500,000-year journey of homo sapiens on Earth, would it be possible to record that event, whatever the medium.

Violet forgot everything and everyone. And since she couldn't manage to say or sing what she was feeling, she simply danced. She danced and danced. She allowed herself to be carried away by the atmosphere, the music, the perfumes. She twirled. She did the splits, remembering, for a few seconds, her ballet classes at the club she went to with her maternal grandmother. She would jump with such lightness that she even surprised the eight-year-old girls. She danced connected and one hundred per cent integrated with everything. It was as if she weighed nothing, because she had just been given a letter of emancipation from the law of gravity. She was graceful and happy. Her feet hardly touched the forest floor. Maybe she had learned from the violets and roses. Who could say?

We rarely reach the state where sounds disappear from the ear and, as if by some mystery, wash over the brain and mind like tsunamis on deserted beaches – without killing anyone, though. It's when the colours of the world and time itself stand still, where they are, and it is no longer they that reach us. It is we who travel happily between the colours and seconds. It was at this moment, which seemed eternal, that something even more unexpected happened.

CHAPTER V

LOVE AND HUNGER

A destabilising tremor preceded the boom that filled the air. That was because the mechanical waves that make sound propagate more quickly in solid elements than in the element of air. The tremor was a great subsonic fruit of the boom.

It was a tremor to uproot plants or sweep you off your feet. It was a boom to make even a volcano block its ears. If volcanoes had ears, that is.

Soon afterwards the air was filled with screeching. Dragons appeared in the sky
with wings four meters wide, and heads the result of a bizarre mix of domestic pig and wild boar. They had squashed faces like pigs, but with huge canine teeth that curved upwards in a complete loop, like those wild mammals from the pig family. They were grunting and squealing terrifyingly. Even the bravest of warriors would feel fear and loathing.

Monkeys looking like a species of baboon rode on their backs. But these had
small curved horns sprouting from between the red hairs on their right and left temples. Each one of them had an instrument like our trumpets – all pointing at the flower dance.

They were also carrying a lot of ammunition composed of enslaved, mutilated notes, packed on the dragons' humped backs. They were the ones feeding the music played by the trumpets.

It was a shock for everyone, and Violet fell and hit her head on a rock. She soon noticed a trickle of blood from above her eyebrow, blurring the vision in her left eye. It was very painful. But this injury hurt far less than the pain and despair that overwhelmed the little girl's heart.

The music being played was from the darkness; it spread death and pain. The poor flowers that didn't have the time or luck to get back to their bases and their roots withered and dried up on the spot. In less than a beat, many daisies were irredeemably divested of their petals. The dragons were swooping above, gaining great height. They swirled in the air, uglifying and clouding the view of the moons, and then they came back ripping through the canopy of the tree tops.

Their number had doubled because another diabolical squadron of that bizarre union of cold-blooded reptiles with warm-blooded mammals had joined them.

Huge, heavy soap bubbles began to fall. They weren't exactly soap bubbles, but were made of pitch. When they burst on the ground or on someone, a sound or very short but loud burst of music resounded in all four corners of the area. It was the end of the unfortunate target, which then splattered and died on the ground– land which, due to the sticky pitch, would remain polluted and barren for decades. These bubbles of heavy ammunition were launched by catapults stationed on the northern limits of the forest, beside the infantry composed of baboons, men and women, beings with the strangest expressions. The men were operating the catapults. The women armed them with the giant bubbles of pitch. And the baboons were beating drums and furnishing the mechanical force for the blasts from the huge bellows making the bubbles.

They wanted to break the defences of the forest to enter with their perfidious instruments. However, the trees joined together. Electric saws operated by the women appeared. It was only later that Violet learned they were brainwashed female slaves. The trees were almost as hard as stone and gave no sign of being felled or cut. They were bleeding, because the sap was their blood. They felt a lot of pain, but they also had their weapons. They released a shower of fruit with melodic seeds that, when sufficient in number, cancelled the effects of the pitch bubbles, making them enter into a rapid process of biodegradation. This was very painful to the ears of the baboons, the men and women – to the point where many of them writhed on the ground. That was when they screamed and voiced words ugly to any ear.

But if at the limits of the forest the battle was more or less even, inside it wasn't one bit balanced. It took some time for the trees in the interior and the plants to able to re-orchestrate themselves and counter-attack. Under their command, the fireflies swarmed together and attacked the dragons' eyes. They hoped to blind them with their firefly lights. Some actually succeeded. But the hatred in the eyes of the dragons was so great that the majority of the lights came out burned. The butterflies could give no help: they were fragile and inspiring, but not good at fighting. But the bees gave the baboons a lot of trouble. The problem was that the baboons' breath was so fetid that it made the bees dazed and confused – so disoriented that they were unable to distinguish the trap of a spider's web from a flower wanting and waiting to be pollinated.

Joaquina and a beautiful black rabbit with lustrous, silky fur dragged Violet to the rabbit's den. The interior trees retuned their leaves and played in the wind, as loud as they could.

The ground, which was shaking because of the malevolent music provided by that aerial attack and bombardment, then began to reverberate a tune similar to the French National anthem, composed by captain Claude Joseph Rouget de Lisle, quartered in Strasbourg, in 1792. It was the revolutionary song known as *La Marseillaise*. All the flowers, plants and insects needed as motivation to confront the tyranny.

If on the physical plane the battle was huge, on the musical plane, it excelled itself. Violet saw almost nothing – and the little she *did* see, she wished she could forget. In the end, the winged dragons and the baboons, hurt and even mutilated, beat a retreat. Even so, they were laughing and celebrating. They said they would be getting drunk to celebrate even more. On the edge of the forest the invading infantry fell back, leaving behind their dead and wounded to rot there along with some fallen trees.

It was time for both armies count their losses. But the damage inside the forest had been much, much worse. Inside there, the battle had been lost.

When Violet recovered and left the den supported by Joaquina and the rabbit Zafira all she saw was dirt, pollution, trees burned inside and out. The poor camellias and night jasmine. The poor daisies, carnations and peace lilies. They were not designed for violence. They were daisies, which lost their petals so easily, and peace lilies, fragile and honourable, which only yearned for harmony. Roses lay on the ground. Some were buds that would never flower. They were like many children on Earth, victims of wars or social violence – evils like the dragons ridden by baboons that dominated the Kingdom of the Seven Moons.

There were some truths that Violet still didn't know, like the connection between the worlds and the inter-relation between people's actions. She knew nothing of the riots caused by fans inside football stadiums, domestic violence, the subjugation of the weakest by the strongest, the cruelty against any animal or plant, bullying, prejudice, ethno-racial conflicts, religious intolerance, and the heinous exterminations that have always ravaged earthly humanity and the other backward worlds of the universe that were all interconnected by an evil desire to generate pain, despair and disease.

Nor did she know that all forms of violence feed each other, no matter how far away they are in space, time or even between dimensions. But Violet *did* know that love and art also form connections of health, hope and happiness, no matter how much distance there is between them. After all, love floods the universe like a constant shower in a tropical forest in Amazonia.

With her little girl's heart, she believed, without being able to explain rationally or with the right words, that, no matter how much hate made souls impermeable, one day love would soften each soul in its own time.

Even so, the pain was immense. The survivors tried to recompose themselves. The pollinating insects began to work avidly. They are a very important part of life's engines on planets or in kingdoms.

In this process of reconstruction, new music was heard. It wasn't joyful, but it brought a message of hope. Joaquina took Violet by the hand and thanked the rabbit, which had to look after its own den. The two left without having to say goodbye to anyone because they were all busy. Just one of the violets, seeing them leaving, said:

"Tell our great mother muse, she has to know. Please summon the Queen."

Joaquina and Violet followed the trail that led to the Marsh of Attraction. As in every journey or adventure, whether through laziness or fear, the first steps are always the most difficult. The forest was dense, but as they walked, the biological and mineral scenario altered. And this beginning of the walk had a further aggravating factor. It was another difficulty in a long journey that lay ahead for a pair of still short legs.

The ground was becoming harder and harder. They stepped on sharp stones, almost cutting their feet. As they walked, they swerved to avoid the many plants with leaves that looked like swords full of long thorns. Violet was angry with the thorns. After all, they were nothing like the soft feel of her teddy bear, which had remained behind entangled in the covers of her cosy bed.

Then she remembered Ibirapuera Park. How good it was to ride a bike along those cycle lanes. She could almost taste the chilled coconut water sold on those hot days in the São Paulo summer. Since she was little she'd played there with her parents. She only had to start throwing popcorn into the lake for the ducks, geese and swans to circle around her. One day, when she was a toddler, she'd run off because her bag of popcorn had been snatched by the insatiable geese, creatures, which, since that day, had been transformed into insolent, rude beings in her opinion.

She also remembered the Planetarium, which imitated the stars in the sky, the many, lovely carp in the Japanese Space, and Manequinho Lopes Park, which was inside Ibirapuera Park, a municipal nursery for flowers, plants and trees. In the centre there's a huge tree, of the species *Phytolacca dioica*, whose roots formed several living wooden divans where you can lie down and look at the birds and flowers. This majestic, magical tree, with its thirty years of life, is a masculine tree whose common name is ombu.

In her memory, words said by her and her parents appeared as if uttered at that moment:

"Daddy! I love this city."

"Who wants an ice-cream with mummy? Ah! Ah! Sit on my lap. Come on!"

"The city should have more parks like this! Let's see if you can catch me. Olé, Catch me if you can."

"No, you catch *me* if *you* can."

But just as waters that have flowed by don't move water mills and also don't quench thirst, the sounds in the memory don't fill ears in the present and don't comfort the now, dominated by an increasingly inhospitable trail.

Two hours later, even from afar, they couldn't see the great baobabs, the mighty oaks. Much less the proud pines, the aromatic eucalyptus trees, the Brazilwood with red sap, the charming araucarias, the rubber trees with the most resistant roots anyone ever thought could exist, and the gigantic sequoias. Majestic.

The dense, dark forest, so impressive for its quantity and improbable diversity of old, wise trees, was behind them, though always present in Violet's heart. She would never forget its aromas of damp wood, tannin, damp earth covered in moss and the perfume of the wild and garden flowers.

She would prefer to forget the rotten smell of war and its dead, whether baboons, dragons or fallen flowers.

Other unknown plant and mineral aromas came one after the other in the air. Happily, the Moons continued to light the arduous way. On a bend, they noticed a stream, born like a babbling, gurgling baby between the rocks and cavities of a grotto

It was the most wonderful water she'd ever had in her life. It quenched the thirst, body's soul's, and washed away the tracks of sad tears that blotted Violet's little face, dirty from earth and blood.

"Thirst, quenched ?????????? Is every river born like this??????????? If they become dirty!!!!!!!! It's because they dirty them!!!!!!!!!!!!!!!!!!!!!!! Every river needs forest along its banks!!!!!!!!!!!! Every forest needs a river running through it!!!!!!!!!!!!! The forests protect the rivers!!!!!!!!!!!!!!!!!!!!!! The rivers water the forests!!!!!!!!!!!!!!!"

Joaquina paused. Then she continued.

"No country on Earth has as much water as your Brazil!!!!!!!!!!!!!! Most of your people don't know how to love their rivers!!!!!!!!!!!!!!!!!!! Tom knew!!!!!!!!!!!!!!!!!!! Men from any country need to learn to love rivers.!!!!!!!!!!!!! Shame on the Blue Earth!!!!! Almost everyone dirties the rivers too much!!!!!!!!!!!!!!!!!! Rivers are the veins through which the blood and sap of the Earth run!!!!!!!!!!!! If it continues like this!!!!!!!!!!!!!!!!!!!!!! The Blue Earth will be called the Land of Dead Rivers!!!!!!!!!!!!!!!!!!!!

"Enough! Enough! Stop!" wailed Violet, and she immediately burst into tears. It was all too much for her. The quaver had become dizzy and bad-tempered because of what had happened and Violet couldn't bear her relentless tirade any longer.

Joaquina got a shock and came to her senses. She was there to look after Violet. To protect and guide her. It wasn't her mission to teach Violet about things related to the environment.

Nor should she have said that in the Kingdom of the Seven Moons the official name for our planet is The Kingdom of the Blue Earth. Incidentally, such a fact is very common, because just as in our world we catalogue and give names to everything and everyone, intelligent beings from other worlds do the same. Therefore, more infinite than the number of worlds in the universe is the number of names to designate these worlds. Much less was it the time to talk about that Tom who loved the forests and rivers. Joaquina was a big fan of the Brazilian composer, Antonio Carlos Brasileiro de Almeida Jobim, better known as Tom Jobim, writer of many wonderful songs that talk about the forests and rivers.

"Come on, my little friend!!!!!!!!!!!!!!!!!!!! Sorry!!!!!!!!!!!!!!!!!! Sorry, come on!!!!!!!

It's incredible how an apology can mend or correct almost anything for a child. No matter how bad the offence or the aggression, often it's enough just to say sorry. Children rarely bear grudges. They just want to be happy.

Violet stopped crying. She looked at the quaver with moist eyes. Her expression was one of a poor, abandoned girl. Her face was one only very little girls can make. And this mortified Joaquina. Violet closed her eyes and let Joaquina wash her face, with its cute button nose, just like Narizinho's[2], once more.

They resumed their journey in silence, which demanded a great deal of effort on the part of Joaquina. She didn't like to stay quiet. Dark clouds covered most of the sky and everything looked more hostile to the eyes of the girl with the German Piano.

Violet was hungry. Very hungry. After all, this was also the first time in her life that there wasn't an adult around asking her to eat. She recalled the desperation of her paternal grandmother whenever she refused to eat for any reason, which could be simply contrariness or that interminable desire to play without interruption which well-fed children have. She also remembered the negotiations that adults and children who are not poor have regarding food, in which the coin of exchange could be a game, a small gift

---

[2] a character (whose name *Narizinho* means 'little nose) from the famous children's book *Sítio do Picapau Amarelo*, written by Brazilian author Monteiro Lobato

or a threat of punishment, like being forbidden to play a video game or use the computer.

And she recalled that when she was just five, one cold Saturday night, when they got back from a pizzeria, her father told her that in her world there were many children who were hungry almost all the time, and that this was very sad. He said that it was more than high time that governments, governors and society attacked misery in the world once and for all. On that same night she thought it was very sad to be a child without food. That it would be the right thing to give the misery in the world a good telling off. But that first they should all go to sleep – and the next day, when they weren't tired, they would then go and find this misery and punish it.

Memories don't fill bellies. Violet was feeling that tiredness and weakness were making her feet drag. It was difficult to go forward. If her mother had been there, she'd certainly have been given a nice mug of hot chocolate and then a hug, with a lap even warmer than the chocolate thrown in for good measure. She would then fall asleep nestled like that, if her mother had been there. However, Joaquina didn't stop, barely wanted to listen to the girl. The urgency of making the journey in safety was more important.

Violet had no choice. Either give it all she had, or stay behind. Maybe the baboon-mounted dragons were still looking for new victims. Fear clouded her tiredness but not her hunger.

Ah, if her mother had been there. Things would be so different. Now the trail pressed on, indifferent to the night, to destinations unknown to her. And now there was no way to go back in time or on the paths trodden up to then.

CHAPTER VI

THE MARSH, THE ORCHIDS AND THE QUICKSANDS

Hours later, the girl from the Kingdom of the Blue Earth was at the end of her strength. They had walked so much on that rocky trail. Her ballet slippers, but for being magic and self-repairing, would have long been in tatters by then. Even so, they didn't afford much protection on such hard, pointy terrain. Her feet were hurting and the little toe on her left foot was swollen and beginning to bleed.

When Violet's knees doubled and hit the ground, Joaquina stopped and didn't even hear the "Oh" coming from the girl's mouth.

"What now?" exclaimed the note.

Violet got up with great difficulty, only to see an intriguing fork in the road. There was a new scenario before them. Different vegetation formed a frightening barrier. It seemed impenetrable, yet inviting. It provoked fear, yet attracted visitors.

Turning right towards the northeast, the terrain seemed to be the easier, more beautiful possible route. There was a gentle descent without insensitive rocks and rough vegetation. It would seduce the eye of anyone because it seemed to be a good, pretty way and a delight to walk on, and also because of a sign fixed at the fork. It was a wooden sign, semi-rotted by time. A magic sign that always read what the traveller wanted to read.

Violet read the following text in silence:

"□□"

Translated into English it read: "Home. The short way home."

A gust of wind ruffled Violet's curly hair. She gave a deep sigh. As if they were racing each other, hope and doubt arrived at the same time in the girl's mind, hindering her thoughts. Then she wanted to follow the sign's directions which, from one second to the next, seemed to blot or even blur the letters written in red, blue and yellow. She longed so much for the way home. But this would be the path to forgetting the mission entrusted to her. A mission she guessed existed, even though she didn't know what it was. Violet felt that her destiny was connected to the destiny of everything and everyone in the Kingdom of the Seven Moons. Even so, something told her she should give up.

"But what will happen to the enslaved notes? The flowers? Will I see the butterflies again? Can I take them home? Can I go home? But how can I help? I'm just a girl!" she pondered, without knowing that if she asked to go home, Joaquina would try to talk her out of it, but in the end the note would have to do what the girl wanted. After all, guardian angels must not subjugate our free will. They can only suggest and protect. But the fallen angels or those who have never flown, no. When they succeed, and if they succeed, they really dominate. They give and change orders without pity or a heavy conscience.

Joaquina remained surprisingly quiet. She looked to the southwest, where the trail led to the high mountains. Some were so high and covered with a blanket of snow coming from the tears of the clouds melting in the chilled air. That would be the shortest way. But would the girl be able to hold up? She had a feeling that they would the fatal victims of the evil army's air force, which was enslaving notes. She was right. The two paths were watched by spies. Especially the one that led to the lonely mountains.

She heard the screeching of dragons. There must have been two of them around – neither far away nor near. Best be careful. That was when the quaver Joaquina noticed the trembling girl, standing up, exhausted and pale. She had passed the reasonable limit for a child who, even in magic clothes, was feeling the cold.

"Is everything OK with you??????????????????"

No reply.

"Are you OK, my little friend?????????????????"

Violet remained silent. Her eyes looked at nothing and seemed to see only the vacuum of despair.

The noise from the dragons indicated that they were on patrol far away. That seemed good. The wind was still strong and the beams from the Seven Moons fought against the heavy clouds. The path had become clearer again.

"The night doesn't seem to want to end, does it??????????? Shall we proceed??????? We don't have much time, my little friend!!!!!!!!!!!!!!!!!!!"

Violet didn't move.

"Let's go, darling!!!!!!!!!!!!!!!!!!"

No movement.

"This won't do!!!!!!!!!!!!!!!!!!You have to help!!!!!!!!!!!!!! Do you want anything???????????"

Violet couldn't manage a word. She just wanted to cry.

She stammered:

"Hungry!" she babbled.

Joaquina knew what to do at once. But she shook her head and changed her mind.

"Come on, little friend, I'll help!!!!!!!!!"

At that moment, the wind carried something different. It was a melody coming from far away. Touch-me-not and princess flower leaves and petals emerged from the mountains. They grouped together shapelessly but after a second glance you could see they looked like a great flowery eagle flying speedily towards Joaquina and Violet, who was now almost fainting.

A light appeared in the eagle's chest and Joaquina bowed with all the ceremonial deference she knew. She lowered her eyes, as if waiting for some advice or warning for something wrong she'd done.

In the centre of the light, Joaquina saw a female, angelic face. The face of a kindly Queen which reprimanded her:

"My dear, you're asking too much of her ∞ ♪ ♫ ♥ !"

"But I only want to help!!!!!!!!!!!!!"

"I know∞ ♪ ♥ ! I know∞ ♥ ! But she's just a child♥ ! Children need special care ♥ ! She's tired ♥ ! You can't demand any more from her♥ !"

"But what do I do????????????"

"You have talents♥ !"

"But I've already used one!!!!!!!!!!!!!! If I use another now there'll only be one left!!!!!!!!! I have to keep them!!!!!!!!!!!!"

"What a terrible way to think ♥ !"

"But if I use them up??????????? And then when I need more, I won't have any!!!!!!!!!!!!"

"My dear, not at all♥! A talent not used at the right time is a talent wasted ♥ ! What's the point of having it and not using it correctly ♥ ? It's as if we never had it ♥ ! We mustn't cast pearls before swine; we mustn't waste the good things we have ♥ ! But if we fail to share with someone the richness of magic, from the heart or from the mind, just when it's most needed, we will never multiply ♥ ! Even the purest water can go bad if it stands still♥ !

"I'm sorry!!!!!!!!!!!!!! I only wanted to do the right thing!!!!!!!!!!!! Oh dear me!!!!!!!"

"I know ♥ ! I know ♥ ! What I told you also goes for material riches ♥ ! Life is always blessed for those who manage to be generous at the right time ♥ !"

"I'll find a way!!!!!!!!!!!!!!!!"

"Do that, dear Joaquina♥ ! I am also at the end of my strength and our conversation has demanded even more of me ♥ ! Goodbye for now, beloved♥ ! God be with you ♫ ♥ !"

The wind scattered the eagle-shaped leaves and petals. The light vanished, along with that most melodious of voices. Joaquina looked at Violet and went towards her.

"Forgive me, my little friend!!!!!!!!!!!! I should have done this a long time ago!!!!!!!!!!"

Lying down, Violet was able to see a movement familiar to her. A movement to release something between the quaver's staff and leg. It was the second tuning fork of the three she carried originally, held in place by a small gold chain. This second one was tuned to A. The same as A on Earth. But like the first one that had dressed Violet, it had something extra. First it sounded A. Then a chord in A major, then another in A minor, only to produce a third chord, this time A seventh.

The sounds from the tuning fork awoke the forest ahead, and it trembled. Out of the blue, the green wall bowed and then there appeared a floating majestic flower. It had the form, texture, colour and appearance of an arum lily. But for its size, that of a giant ice cream glass, those that can fit 5 scoops, and its admirable content, it was identical to the arum lilies we know.

The flower floated over to Violet's face and hovered in mid-air. Joaquina helped her to hold the flower cup to drink. What an incredible liquid! The first gulp was warm and creamy, the second chilled like milk and ice cream. And the third, coffee with whipped cream. The fourth, believe it or not, was water melon juice!

That special milk was able to understand the mind of anyone who drank it and alter the flavour according to the desires and necessities of the drinker. There were just two things it couldn't imitate: hot chocolate made by Violet's mother and mother's milk from bears, she-wolves, whales, lionesses, gazelles, tigresses, groundhogs, otters, and women.

However, the main thing about that succulent drink wasn't its taste but the health and sustenance it gave. The liquid went down Violet's throat and soon filled her stomach, which ached with hunger. What a lovely sensation of warmth, what peace! In a short time the magic milk was being digested, then to be absorbed in the intestines and flow through Violet's blood supply. Her wounds and bruises healed quickly. A new strength flooded through her. Violet was a normal girl. A girl full of energy, wanting to run, dance, play all the time. But as this was neither the time nor the place, she kept her energy to herself. She just got up and said:

"I feel great now! Thank you! Thank you, lady flower!!!!!!!!!"

While the arum lily floated off, Violet jumped up and down and hugged Joaquina, smacking her cheeks with kisses.

"What's this?????!!!!!!!!!! Stop that!!!!!!!!!!!!!!"

"I'm happy!"

"Imagine if you weren't!!!!!!!!!!!!!!!!!!"

Joaquina was calmer now. She knew that in this kingdom the food would provide a human with the necessary nourishment for at least fifteen days. It contained all the vitamins, minerals and proteins that a girl, a zebra or even a whale calf needed. Besides this, it was an incredible combination of simple and complex carbohydrates. If one of the top nutritionists were to analyse it, they would be puzzled by the formulation – there were also extra-super complex carbohydrates and natural fibres. Incredible? Extraordinary? Not so much. After all, it was magic milk from the arum lilies in the Kingdom of the Seven Moons, and life always produces the right food, when necessary, to sustain life itself.

"Better??????????? Good, good!!!!!!!!!!!!!!!!!!!!!"

"Maybe the best route would be the path to the northeast," Joaquina said, while she heard from Violet:

"No!"

The girl puffed out her chest, breathing in a great deal of courage from the air, as if she wanted to expel the fear. Although the courage had managed to enter her child's lungs, the fear resisted and stayed there, squeezed and hidden in an alveolus in the left lung. As soon as it could, it would act again to invade the girl's heart.

Then she exclaimed.

"Let's go! We're going to win! We'll do it! Our father in Heaven will help the notes and flowers! Won't he?" said Violet.

"That's the ticket, little heroine!!!!!!!!!! I knew you wouldn't lose heart!!!!!!!!!! My musical knight in armour!!!!!!!!!!!!!!!!!!! Let's get going, warrior with a baton!!!!!!!!!!!!!!!!!!!"

"Baton? What do you mean, warrior with a baton?"

Joaquina made up her mind. The chosen route was not the northeast, much less the southwest. Six steps ahead, they were off the trail, heading into the dense forest. The Second Moon was at its zenith in the heavenly dome: it was the full moon phase and its orange beams were very strong. They broke through the cover of heavy clouds, and fell like tiny orange flecks of glitter, lighting the way. The high wind, the one that blows at an altitude above five-thousand meters, also helped to disperse them. Joaquina and Violet went ahead blessing that strong moonlight. They were in the Marsh of Love, which had many other names such as the Marsh of Sensuality, the Marsh of Twin Souls, the Marsh of Lovers etc. They were in the Marsh also called the Marsh of Passions, the Marsh of Seduction, the Marsh of Eternal Love, and even the Marsh of the Fount of Female and Male Life.

The name changed according to the mental state of the adventurer who ventured into it. However, through pure logic and good sense, this marsh had no name for Violet. After all, she was a child and, therefore, it was not yet her time to encounter perils or experience happiness there. Even so, she felt intuitively that she was uncovering fascinating, mysterious and adventurous trails there.

She could feel, but without being affected, the atmosphere filled with pheromones. She didn't know what they were, nor was she interested in knowing. Her curiosity was in fact drawn to the new flowers that were sprouting in the most unlikely places. At the same time, her misgivings were focused on the trail.

"Be careful!!!!!!!!!!!!! The most beautiful orchids are born here!!!!!!!!! And it's here that the most dangerous quicksands are born."

'Quicksands? What's quicksand?"

'Nowhere else are such fascinating flowers born!!!!!!!!!!!! Or such dangerous trails!!!!!!!!!!!!!!!

Her friend's ambiguous reply rang alarm bells for the girl. She clung to Joaquina and moved not even one millimetre away from her.

The cicadas were singing. Their voices were as high as those of sopranos in arias from operas about love. The frogs were croaking and the crickets were chirping incessantly. There were pools, lakes and rivers that mixed their waters at every moment. Some shallow, others deep. Some muddy, others crystal clear. Many hid sharp, rotten branches that could hurt a swimmer who didn't know they were there. Others had dense, dark sludge at the bottom, though it was medicinal, healing mud – especially if the wound was one of the heart. But, depending on where it was, the sludge could trap and perhaps even drown anyone unfortunate to sink their feet in it.

Could there be giant crocodiles in those waters? Were there boa constrictors or poisonous snakes lying in wait for the careless traveller? Huge tarantulas wove their enormous webs here and there. Centipedes, whose name should more precisely be "ducentipedes" or "trecentipedes," were strong enough to fight the tarantulas and were rarely devoured by them. This was not the case with the cicadas. If they were out of tune, they were easy targets – their only protection was to sing in tune so that the tarantulas would become docile. As for the plants, there was almost no way of telling which were carnivorous or not. If some were big enough to swallow even an elephant with ease, imagine a man! However, it was exactly inside some of these that happiness and the vital force pulsated at will. In this marsh, everything that was mineral, vegetal, animal and human was an attraction. Everything could be scary or fascinating. It depended on the traveller's point of view. The fear or fascination was generated by the lenses or iris of the person looking.

The marsh was also the possible home for many nymphs, fairies, and beings equivalent to the satyrs in Greek mythology. There are those who say that the inspiration for such Greek myths as those about Aphrodite and Dionysus, have their source in the Marsh of Love. It is highly likely that William Shakespeare, the greatest writer and poet in the English language, and also the most influential dramatist in the history of the Earth, born on April 23 in the small English town of Stratford-upon-Avon, had drunk from its springs in his sleep in order to write one of his masterpieces, "A Midsummer Night's Dream".

Violet and Joaquina pressed on, avoiding stepping on any suspicious, not solid terrain. But it was impossible not to get wet in the waters and not to fall in love with the orchids and exotic flowers. The marsh was also musical. At times you could hear music in double time, with the first beat strongly accentuated and with growing modulation. It sounded like *Habanera* from the opera "Carmen," by French composer Georges Bizet. Other times, the music became angelic, and not sensual, like the previously mentioned music. But for sure all forms of music that talk about sublime love, platonic love or carnal love were composed there and performed at the same time.

In that marsh, more and more melodies about passion, solitude and jealousy sounded and resonated. In that marsh, for anyone who had ears to listen, even the unimaginable music of Orpheus for Eurydice could be appreciated. And just as in the Greek myth – where Orpheus's music calmed beasts and shook the kingdom of Hades to conquer death temporarily, in the attempt to save his beloved Eurydice– in that marsh the music of love could do anything.

They hadn't covered half of the way yet and, although she didn't understand the meaning of everything there, Violet didn't want to leave. Joaquina was also a bit strange. Her determination to proceed with the mission seemed to diminish.

That was when an imposing lady conductor, three metres tall, appeared, stopping all the music. She was more beautiful and graceful than any ballerina, shapelier and prettier than any Miss Universe. Her long, shiny, golden hair was also her clothes. Her eyes were blue, but suddenly turned turquoise, only to turn black like the depths of the sea, then blue again. Her skin tone also changed smoothly, going from ebony black to shades known and unknown.

But if her appearance was impressive, her voice would silence anyone. She had the highest, clearest voice ever heard. However, that voice could become strong and deep, like the best tenors, though without losing its timbre of femininity.

Her words brooked no questioning. There was no power of reasoning, however intelligent or persuasive, that could question her. After all, love is sublime, love is the lord and also the lady. You don't question love!

Violet and Joaquina were standing before the muse and Fairy Queen of the Marsh of Love. Now they just wanted to look at her. They yearned ardently to hear her and adore her, as poet Vinicius de Moraes once wrote in his *Soneto de Fidelidade* (Sonnet of Fidelity)

> "*.........Let it not be not immortal, since it is flame*
> *But let it be infinite while it lasts*"

> "*......Que não seja imortal, posto que é chama*
> *Mas que seja infinito enquanto dure.*"

CHAPTER VII

ILLUSIONS, SIREN SONGS AND THE PATHS OF DESTINY

The melody emerging from the fleshy, well-defined lips of the Fairy Queen of the
Marsh was sublime and delightful. It sparked an inner fire and a purity typical of the calm that comes after the tempestuous collisions of the waves breaking against huge coastal rocks on stormy days.

But, if she could, Joaquina would have chosen to be deaf at that moment. Quite deaf. Simply not to have to face the powerful summons for her attention that the music carried. Whereas Violet was smiling and couldn't understand a word the fairy said. With her ingenuous look and expression she just heard adorable music which would contribute so much in the future to her emotional and physical health as an adult. Through the purest magic, one got told off, the other got a gift. Who could understand how this was possible? After all, if women are already wonderful, complex creatures, imagine Fairy Queens! They can do things even the imagination could never imagine.

Just like the conversation with the flower eagle, before heading for the marsh, this was also a dialogue very difficult to translate into any human language. So, the partial, imprecise transcript goes more or less like this:

"Irresponsible ō § Q ♥ ♫ ♫ ♥! Very irresponsible ō § Q ♥ ♫ ♫ ♥! Children have to be loved and protected ō § Q ♥ ♫ ♫ ♥! You should never have brought her here ō § Q ♥ ♫ ♫ ♥! Now is not the time, it's too soon for her, you knew that ō § Q ♥ ♫ ♫ ♥!"

Joaquina was bold enough to try to explain:

"But!!!!!!!!!!!!!! But, Majesty!!!!!!!!!!!!!! I thought it wouldn't be a problem!!!!!!!!!!!!"

This was an unfortunate attempt that just made the situation worse.

"And it wasn't in the end ō § Q ♥ ♫ ♫ ♥! But that wasn't because of you ō § Q ♥ ♫ ♫" ♥!

"But the road was very dangerous !!!!!!!!!!!!!!!!!!!!" retorted Joaquina to the fairy.

"It was indeed ō § Q ♥ ♫ ♫ ♥!"

"But she wasn't going to manage it!!!!!!!!!!!!!!!!!!!" insisted the note.

'Maybe she wouldn't have managed it at all ō § Q ♥ ♫ ♫ ♥! Maybe she'd even have given up ō § Q ♥ ♫ ♫ ♥! Even so, children have to be protected, not exposed ō § Q ♥ ♫ ♫ ♥! There are no shortcuts in life ō § Q ♥ ♫ ♫ ♥! Early eroticization does them harm, a lot of harm ō § Q ♥ ♫ ♫ ♥!"

"But I thought that if we passed through here very quickly, there'd be no problem!!!!!!!!!!!!"

"You cannot behave like certain music that went to the Kingdom of the Blue Earth, which wants to cut childhood short before its time ō § Q ♥ ♫ ♫ ♥! After they discovered how much money they could make with children, many people began to create products and services just to make money, without thinking if that would harm them or not ō § Q ♥ ♫ ♫ ♥! There's a lot of good music for children but the amount of utter rubbish is intolerable ō § Q ♥ ♫ ♫ ♥!"

"But????????????????"

"But nothing ō § Q ♥ ♫ ♫ ♥! The Field of Sexuality is divine. It's vital for life itself. It is the most powerful creative force after the great force ō § Q ♥ ♫ ♫ ♥! But everything has its time ō § Q ♥ ♫ ♫ ♥! Children should learn about anatomy, sexuality and everything else that constitutes life ō § Q ♥ ♫ ♫ ♥! But calmly ō § Q ♥ ♫ ♫ ♥! It is not right to expose them and throw them into this before their minds and bodies are ready ō § Q ♥ ♫ ♫ ♥!"

"I'm sorry!!!!!!!!!!!!!!!!!!!! I didn't throw her into anything !!!!!!!!!!!!!!!!!!!!"

"But you went too far ō § Q ♥ ♫ ♫ ♥! She's not supposed to be here now ō § Q ♥ ♫ ♫ ♥! It was I who covered her ears and eyes ō § Q ♥ ♫ ♫ ♥! In my kingdom there are several sub-kingdoms ō § Q ♥ ♫ ♫ ♥! Some are Edens, others purgatories ō § Q ♥ ♫ ♫ ♥! There are also caramel orchards, honey pools, ice-cream flowers, strawberry and chocolate houses, puffs of soft clouds where you can lie down and dream, and also holes where even the light blesses itself before entering ō § Q ♥ ♫ ♫ ♥! I don't even want to mention the Valley of the Energy Sick, the Lake of the Drunk, far less the Well of the Usurpers of the Sexuality of Others ō § Q ♥ ♫ ♫ ♥!"

"But, but, but!!!!!!! We were going to steer well clear of all that!!!!!!!!!!"

"If I didn't know that I would already have struck you dead ō § Q ♥ ♫ ♫ ♥!"

"But, but, but!!!!!!!!!!"

"But, nothing ō § Q ♥ ♫ ♫ ♥! It is correct that you are almost at the edge of the marsh, though it is perilous for her ō § Q ♥ ♫ ♫ ♥!

At that instant, the Fairy Queen's tone of voice boomed like the rumble of mysterious

thunder, and she grew even taller! She became pale and then went red. Joaquina would never again witness such a severe expression. But Violet just went on listening, seeing something gentle and pure.

"As I've already said, ō § Q ♥ ♫ ♫ ♥! Little ones must be loved and protected ō § Q

♫ ♫ ♥! Never used for money, gratuitous entertainment or even worse things ō § Q ♥ ♫ ♫ ♥! I do not accept this ō § Q ♥ ♫ ♫ ♥! Love children ō § Q ♥ ♫ ♫ ♥! I cannot tolerate those who exploit them. For these people I have the most terrible quicksands that swallow everything, even the depths of their rotten souls ō § Q ♥ ♫ ♫ ♥!"

The musical note trembled all over. She turned into a jelly baby or a very, very soft toasted marshmallow. However, whether through fear or raised awareness, she came to her senses. She realized how much she'd put at risk. In a cold sweat, she lowered her head in shame. It hadn't been bad intentions or laziness, but an error of judgment. It had been a good intention that went wrong. She couldn't look the Fairy Queen in the face.

She simply wanted to say "I'm sorry". She couldn't. The energy radiated by the fairy was too much. It ached without causing pain, froze without going cold and didn't hurt. But no one would want to approach or be approached by her even for a second.

Joaquina tried to babble an apology. She also failed at this task. As there was nothing else to be done, she tried to stay quiet. Would she manage? There was no time to find out. The Fairy Queen of the Marsh of Love noticed her sincere remorse at that same moment. She went back to her original size.

Her voice would no longer shake the foundations of a mountain, but rather would enchant even the deafest fish which, actually, don't hear very well anyway. She could light the way for the blindest mole. But what she actually did was to transmit the priceless sensation that Joaquina was forgiven and would have another chance.

The music that followed this was very powerful. It no longer spoke of love or any manifestation of it. It spoke of something angelic and childlike. A swarm of leaves and fireflies enveloped Joaquina and Violet. A carpet of the same living material took shape, and when they least expected it, the swarm pushed them onto the carpet, which took off in flight. An energetic, vigorous flight. They flew over the treetops, and then ascended at a very steep angle. An extreme angle. They reached ten thousand metres. The carpet did a manoeuvre, in aviation called a loop, and passed in front of the Second Moon from the perspective of someone looking from the ground. Then it flew inverted, that is to say upside down, which pilots call negative G force, where G means gravity acceleration. But for the swarm of leaves and fireflies holding them, the two would have fallen off the carpet.

The Marsh of Love was different when seen from above. They saw it as even more beautiful. It was gigantic almost infinite in complexity and creativity. Energised vapours emanated from it, travelling in time and space and also between dimensions to inflame desire in all species, with a view to the necessary procreation. Ectoplasms of amorous and sensual desire in colours of lilac, pink, blue, orange and red appeared in the sky in the shape of twisting tornados, and from there proceeded through time, space and dimensions to help and feed the eternal mission of the cupids and gods of love in each world or kingdom.

The carpet and the rookie aviators did a corkscrew manoeuvre and then carried on at high speed, almost scraping the treetops.

"Woohoo! Amazing! Do it again! Way-hay! Great! Wow! Woohoo"

"Take it easy!!!!!!!!!!!!!!!!!!!!!!!!!!!"

"Woohoo! Do it again. Again. Again!"

"Take it easy!!!!!!!!!!!!!!!!!!!!"

Soon the carpet and the swarm of flowers and fireflies landed gently at the same crossroads where, some time before, the two had gone into the marsh.

"Who was she?"

"Don't worry about that!!!!!!!!!!!!!!! One day you'll know!!!!!!!!!!!!!!!!"

"She's so nice. What's her name?"

"She has many!!!!!!!!!!!!!! It depends on the language, the culture, the world!!!!!!!!!!!!!!!! Some are more precise, others not so much, like Kurupi or even the Queen of the Waters!!!!!!!!!!!!!!!!!!!!!!!!"

"What do you mean, it depends on the world?"

"I mean it depends on the world!!!!!!!!!!! There are many names in yours: Aphrodite, Venus Parvati, Sjofn, Aine of Knockaine etc!!!!!!!!!!!!!!!!!!!!!!!!!!!!!!"

The reply didn't interest and much less satisfy the childish curiosity that didn't want to know about the myths, mythologies, goddesses and religions of the variety of people on Earth. So Violet's attention was easily distracted. Looking ahead and scratching her head with her right hand, she noticed that the carpet was slowly beginning to take off again.

"Thank you dear carpet! Thank you leaves! Thank you fireflies! It was wonderful!"

The carpet seemed to bow to her. In the middle of its flowery body a face with a friendly expression appeared and smiled at Violet. The carpet and the swarm went back to where they had started out and then Joaquina led Violet along the trail heading southwest.

When the first rays of the Sun came to flirt with the night-owl beams from the Seven Moons, the landscape became even more beautiful. Dawn broke and hopes were reborn.

"Daytime at last!!!!!!!!!!!!!!!!!!!!!!!"

"How lovely!"

"I thought the shades of night would never end!!!!!!!!!!!!!!!!!!!!!!!!!!!!!!!"

Joaquina heard the song of many birds. One of them, a kiskadee, brought some important information from afar, a strong, opportune message of hope.

"Hurrah!!!!!!!!!!!!! The nights are so nice!!!!!!!!!!! I don't like the dark!!!!!!!! Night and the dark are not the same thing!!!!!!!!!!!!!!!!!!! Tonight was decisive!!!!!!!!!!!!!!!! By the looks of things, they lost!!!!!!!!!!!!"

Violet widened her eyes, and, with furrowed brow, pretended to understand the gravity of the situation explained by Joaquina. In the kingdom of the Seven Moons, the nights were getting longer and longer and, consequently, the days too. And this was happening because of a strategy that smelt fishy. A diabolical, implausible plan by the oppressive musical forces.

It was diabolical because its objective was slavery. It was implausible because it wouldn't work and would result in the loss of everything.

Even for the very architects of the senseless rotational imbalance aimed for by the strategy. The wretched oppressive forces believed that if they stopped the rotation of the planet around its own axis, they would cause eternal night on one side and endless day on the other. This way, the nocturnal combat would be a reinforcement of the dark forces. Although the nights are blessed and the dark forces are not, it is precisely during the night that the latter can move around with more agility. They reckoned that if they were successful in stopping the rotation of the planet, a part of the Kingdom of the Seven Moons would practically freeze over while the other would toast in the scorching sun. They intended to conquer half of the Kingdom and lose the other to the infernal heat. As they could not have the whole Kingdom, they were trying to have at least half of the Kingdom of the Seven Moons.

How were they doing this? Simple. A long time beforehand, they had gathered together all the perverse magic they knew, with the help of diabolical spirits, which penetrated the spiritual heart of Kingdom of the Seven Moons and made it sick. It was already pulsating more slowly. On the physical plane, well below the tectonic plates of the Kingdom of the Seven Moons, vibrated an anti-music, deep and deaf to almost all ears – this sound also decelerated the angular speed of the Planet or Kingdom of the Seven Moons.

It was a malign, brutal and stupid plan. It would generate an unimaginable disaster, because in all the worlds the climate depends on a complex and almost infinite set of factors, such as the level of solar activity, distance from the Sun, inclination of the planetary axis, number of moons or natural satellites, period of rotation around the axis, level of volcanic activity, the amount of frozen water at the poles, the volume of water in the oceans, sea currents etc. It also depends on the size and position of the continents, the height of mountain ranges and chains, concentration of greenhouse gases, the health and diversity of the flora and even the number of flowers and butterflies. The climate is a living organism that needs to be healthy to sustain the maximum quantity and diversity of life possible.

The insensitivity and perversity of the oppressive forces were limitless. If they were successful in this egotistical enterprise, the habitat that they knew would alter so radically that life and the sources of music, including their very selves, would be extinct.

The catastrophic consequences of this evil were already noticeable. Many coastal regions were suffering from increasingly devastating tsunamis. Even the biosphere was showing signs of becoming feverish and sick. The rains were becoming torrential and periods of droughts longer and longer. Earthquakes were more frequent because of subterranean detonations of the most powerful acid music. These explosions were creating an effect like the atomic bombs in our world which, besides cracking the tectonic structures, leave a radioactive trace of anti-life.

Happily, in this intention, the oppressive musical forces were frustrated by the Greater Power, because this could never happen. Thus, the Father and Mother of everything and everyone intervened and cut this plan at the roots, ordering that the forces that protect the worlds and dimensions put an immediate stop to the plan. That was when the Seven Moons compensated for the rotational imbalance, reinforcing planetary interaction. By means of an invisible, but very powerful, gravitational sling they were already synchronizing the days and nights of the Kingdom of the Seven Moons once more. Divine angels penetrated the Kingdom's heart, drove out the demons and cured it, restoring the previous healthy pulsation.

In no time at all, the climatic changes would be reverted and the battles between the musical forces would occur on a living, not a condemned planet. This was the wonderful news brought by the young kiskadee, who had got it from the beak of a humming bird, which for its part, had heard the good news from a bromeliad planted in a distant tropical forest. This was also Joaquina's explanation to Violet.

"Long live the little planet! Little planet! Little planet". The girl shouted and began to began to twirl on tiptoe.

"What's this???????? You don't understand anything!!!!!!!!!!!!!!!!!!!!!!"

"Yes I do. That's not fair at all. Long live everyone!"

Violet continued to celebrate and ran off along the trail. There is no holding back a well-fed eight-year-old girl who is happy. Joaquina ran after her and took the lead. After all, she was the one who should be the guide.

The two ran the first six kilometres of the trail in half an hour. Then, at a quick walking pace, their average speed fell from twelve kilometres an hour to five, and then to four. The climb was getting steeper and steeper. Though out of breath, Violet didn't seem tired, didn't have cramp and didn't want to stop.

Joaquina put the brakes on for the two of them. The path was narrow and the abyss greater and greater.

"Careful here!!!!!!!!!!!!!!!!! It's slippery!!!!!!!!!!!!!!!!!"

Violet noticed a rock falling at the side of the trail. It took fifty-two seconds for them to hear the first sounds of it hitting the ground. They continued their climb, which now skirted a huge mountain. The wind was biting more. They began to tread on ground made white from a blanket of snow that became softer and deeper as they gained altitude.

This trail led them to a bridge made of rope and wood. Girl and note crossed hand in hand, when suddenly one of the planks on the bridge split.

"Ahhhhhhhhhhhhhhhh!" screamed Violet, feeling nothing under her feet.

The world seemed to shake and accelerate upwards. In fact, it was she who was beginning to fall. But for Joaquina's quick reflex action, Violet would have plummeted into the abyss.

"Hold tight!!!!!!!!!!!!!!!! I've got you!!!!!!!!!!!!!!!!!!Come up to me !!!!!!!!!!!!!!!! Come up to me!!!!!!!!!!!!!!!!!!!!!!!!! Come on, you can do it!!!!!!!!!!!!!!!"

The girl was hanging in the air, held by the tiny hand of the note, which little by little was taking on human form.

"Aaaah!"

"Come on!!!!!!!!!!!!!!!!!"

"Aaaaaaaah!!!!!!!!!!"

"No crying, now!!!!!!!!!!!!!!!!!! Come on!!!!!!!!!!!!!!!!!!"

The bridge had been exposed to the rigours of time and, not being maintained for ages, was very fragile. How long could it sustain that swinging caused by the struggle to keep a girl of 30kg from certain death?

The creaking of ropes against the pieces of wood that made up the bridge could be clearly heard. This was not a good sign. Unwanted sounds generated by the screech of winged dragons ricocheted, echoing against the rock walls. They were patrolling the area not very far away. Would they arrive soon? Were they approaching or pulling back? The fear locked away up to then in a small corner of Violet's lung grew and turned into panic. It was almost fatal. Her nervous system collapsed. The medulla wasn't transmitting electric command impulses to the muscles to save her. It simply froze. It stiffened her muscles as if she were an old woman with arthrosis.

"Be brave"!!!!!!!!!!!!!!!!!!!!!!"

"Aaaagh!!!!!!!!!!!!!!!!!!"

Joaquina made a phenomenal effort. She managed to hoist Violet up and also had to drag her for the remaining fifty metres of bridge to get them to the other side. The two of them collapsed. One through total panic. The other through total exhaustion.

Forty minutes later, Violet opened her eyes and saw a quaver dripping frozen sweat. She could never have imagined that in this world musical notes were made in part of water, and that, therefore, they sweated in fear, emotion or from the heat.

"Thank you!" she said with the greatest tenderness she could, while wiping the ice crystals from her friend's face. Joaquina woke up coughing. She got up and noticed she was limping. She had distended her leg.

"Crikey!!!!!!!!!!!!!!!!!!!! You're supposed to help !!!!!!!!!!!!!!!!!!!!"

"Sorry!"

"I've never seen anyone freeze like that!!!!!!!!!!"

"Thank you for saving my life!"

Violet hugged Joaquina and gave her a kiss. Only someone who has received the spontaneous kiss of a child, overflowing with tenderness, can understand what Joaquina felt. Only those who have one day felt the touch, warmth and smell of a child's body asking for protection and at the same time giving affection know what we're talking about here. Joaquina wanted to be as incredible, nice and strong as Violet thought she was. This had never happened to her. The confidence placed in Joaquina by the girl triggered in her an immense desire to go above and beyond. To be a note on the side of good. She would give her own life to protect Violet. Joaquina was not aware that one of the many reasons for the existence of children in every world is to ignite in adults the desire to be better than they really are.

A joy she'd never felt before flooded her soul.

"Let's go my little friend!!!!!!!!!!!!!!! The dragons must be nearby!!!!!!!!!!!!!! We have no time to lose!!!!!!!!!!!!!!!!!!!!"

"Are you alright?"

"Yes!!!!!!!!!!"

"Is your leg hurting?"

"No!!!!!!!!!!!!!! No!!!!!!!!!!!!!!! Everything's ok!!!!!!!!!!!!!!!!

"Why are you limping?"

"Sometimes I like to limp!!!!!!!!!!!!!!"

Violet laughed. She might be ingenuous, but she was no fool.

"Ah! That's a good one. I like to limp...I like to limp…I like that."

On this other side of the mountain range the ravine was even deeper. Because of the direction of the wind and the topographical characteristics, the trail on this side had no snow drifts. Violet was hoping that at the next bend there would be a short cut or a path down the mountain. This was soon in coming.

"Look there's a path down there as well."

"But the way is up!!!!!!!!!!!!!!"

"But it looks so nice down there."

"We're going up!!!!!!!!!!!!!! It's very dangerous down there!!!!!!!!!!!!!!!!"

"Alright," Violet grumbled, controlling a strong desire not to obey her protector's advice.

They stopped when it was almost midday. There was no way to go forward. The trail had collapsed and, because of the great distance, it was not possible to jump. They were frozen to the bone because of the cold. What were they to do?

"Let's go back and go down by the other path?

"Out of the question!!!!!!!!!!!! I've learnt that there are no short cuts in life!!!!!!!!!!!!!!"

Violet didn't understand, but neither did she question Joaquina. She just looked horrified. Between the mountains she could see two dragons flying in hunting formation, heading straight for them. She let out a terrified squeal:

"Over there Joaquina, look!"

Joaquina's mind speeded up as never before. There had to be a way out. They couldn't have made so much effort for nothing. The winged reptiles were getting nearer, and with them, fear too. She decided to get the last magic tuning fork. Would she use it or not? Seen in the light of day, the dragons, with their pig/wild boar faces, seemed even more repulsive.

"Jeepers! What now?"

Violet was about to use the last tuning fork when she saw a small opening just a metre above them, a cave, about eighty centimetres in diameter. They'd been so disheartened by the disappearance of the trail, and terrified at the sight of the dragons, that they simply had not looked up.

"We can climb up there!!!!!!!!!!!!!!! You get on top of my head!!!!!!!!!!! And then pull me up!!!!!!!!!!!!!!! Are you going to freeze???????????????"

"No! I won't freeze!"

That's what they did. First Violet, standing on Joaquina's head, climbed up, getting a grip on the thinnest cracks in the rocks of the rock wall and flung herself into the cave. She turned around and stretched out both arms to pull up her friend. She found the strength thanks to the combination of courage and fear.

Curled up, the two hugged each other inside the cave, not even wanting to open their eyes. One of the dragons got a good whiff of human – they have an excellent sense of smell. It did an almost acrobatic twist and went back to the interrupted trail. The baboon on its back whistled to the second dragon and its horned primate rider. The dragon managed to land with great difficulty on the narrow trail. Its enormous size meant that it had to constantly flap its brown wings so as not to fall. The other circled around the area. Then its baboon rider spoke (its speech sounded like someone about to vomit):

"Aaaargh!!!! What's this? The path's closed. Nobody could be there."

The first baboon grumbled, trying to see what its dragon was sniffing at the entrance to the cave:

"Get your big head out of the way, you stupid dragon. Let me see inside."

Tucked away like two creatures in their den, Violet and Joaquina squeezed themselves into the back of the cave while the great stinking face blocked the light at the entrance. It sniffed and searched. It drooled and sneezed wet vapours that were soon condensed in the cold of that altitude. The darkness of the cave would protect them from being seen by the dragon until it got accustomed to the difference in light between the back of the cave and the outside world. But if they were temporarily saved from being seen by the dragon, its pig/wild boar sense of smell had already detected them.

"Eeeeh! This dragon of yours must have sniffed so much *coorraína* that its nostrils have rotted. Eeeeh!" squealed the second baboon.

"It's *mardita* taken with a lot of *mamanguaça* that kills. Eeeeh!" it continued, bellowing. *Mamanguaça* was a kind of rum made from toxic mushrooms, whose alcohol by volume level was almost 72%. The term *mardita* was another name for *coorraína*, a drug that had been produced for two hundred years in the Kingdom of the Seven Moons. This drug was used to make the evil armies excited and fearless. Its devastating effect on mental and physical health was similar to the effects of crack and cocaine in the Kingdom of the Blue Earth. If taken together with *mamanguaça*, then it increased its potential and negative effects – after this point of dependency, there was almost no possibility of regeneration for the spirit and body. But the oppressive forces of music were not one bit concerned about this. All that interested them were targets and results.

"Move over, useless imbecile and let me see," said the first baboon, letting go of the reins and jumping over its dragon's neck. He punched the animal in the head and bawled at top volume:

"Let me see! Seeeee! I've already asked you once, damn you"

Another punch landed below the chin. The dragon had a strong neck but even so, it must have hurt. It hung its strange face to the right and its rider scaled the rest of the rock wall to enter the cave. Joaquina did not allow herself to be overcome by fear. She jumped with everything she could, digging one of her pointed legs into one of the baboon's eyes.

It was fatal. Taken by surprise, the baboon made an abrupt retreat. One of the dragon's wings brushed by him. He began to fall. However, he had the reflexes and presence of mind to grab Joaquina by the leg and she would have fallen too if she hadn't been holding onto the ridges in the cave walls.

That was when the dragon's claws slid and, unbalanced, it came away from the smooth mountain rock. It lost altitude and fell, flapping its wings. More or less one hundred metres further down, it recovered and started flying again.

The baboon and quaver would have had the shared the same fate as the dragon, but, this time, there was an indignant little girl at the epicentre of the action. She didn't freeze in panic. Driven more by instinct than rationality, Violet sprang up like a cat and grabbed Joaquina by the head.

"Get away you horrible creature! She's my friend!"

Pulled this way and that, Joaquina moaned, twisting her mouth:

"Aaaaaaaaaaaaaaagh!!!!!!!!!!!!!!"

The baboon, with one eye bleeding and taken by surprise by the jolt from the sudden deceleration of the anchored Joaquina, couldn't hold on. Despite having very strong nails, fingers and fists, it let go of Joaquina's leg. It plummeted only to end its miserable existence in a place inaccessible to good beings. It fell to a place impenetrable by those who wish to sleep without having nightmares.

The second baboon and its dragon drew away in a cowardly fashion to warn their war command. And they would never tell the true story of how they had been defeated. They would swear they had been surprised by a task force so numerous that they had beaten a retreat. Evil doers are only brave when they think they have the advantage. But they die of shame if they have to admit this to anyone, mainly to their cronies.

"Now it's my turn to thank you!!!!!!!!!!!!!!!!!! I thought I'd be left with no neck!!!!!!!!!!!!" said Joaquina, inclining her head from side to side, imitating MMA fighters in the Kingdom of the Blue Earth.

"We taught him a lesson, didn't we?"

"A good one!!!!!!!!!!!!!! A really good one!!!!!!!!!!!!!! Yeah! Now my neck's hurting too!!!!!! But we have to be quick!!!!!!!!!!!!!!!! Now they know about us!!!!!!!!!!!!!!!!!"

The sun hadn't yet appeared at its zenith. Violet and Joaquina looked like two eagle chicks abandoned by their parents. They didn't know how to fly and looked over the edge of the rock wall to the immensity of the icy mountains. Their eyes were fixed on the ruined stretch of trail. Instinctively they calculated the distance and trembled just thinking about trying to jump it. Violet turned her delicate little neck upwards. The vertical rock wall was smooth, damp and looked like a giant puffing out his chest challengingly, wanting to say in an archaic language and in a slow chant in deep tones:

"Come and face me, come on! Just try to climb me. I'll have your lives. Lives that will erode on my walls. Erosion, how erosion hurts, I want a remedy for erosion. It hurts me so much to erode. I don't want to erode any more. I'm going to erode you too."

In that cold, and faced with such an impasse, Violet wanted to suggest going back. But she didn't dare say it, and kept her thoughts to herself. Joaquina inspected the back of the cave, in the hope of finding a passage that would free them. She looked, felt and searched. She even scraped her legs on the frozen, wrinkled rocks. Nothing! The cave was embedded in the solid rock. Probably the hardest and most resistant rock that existed in that Kingdom. The girl went on inspecting the outside world. Her neck never stopped turning from one side to the other, making her abundant curls hang on the opposite side to the movement. Suddenly, Joaquina pointed at something:

"Look there!"

Heavy, dark clouds covered the top of the rock wall. It began to rain. Little by little the rain became hail, then flakes of snow appeared, pushed forward mercilessly by the wind that was blowing hard. The temperature dropped by six degrees in less than two minutes. It must have been close to minus two, but the thermal sensation was equivalent to a drop of thirty degrees.

In silence, Violet and Joaquina looked at the mountains, which seemed to have human features. They were severe, rough and angry expressions. The wind was whistling through the ravines like air blown through the great flutes of Tibetan monks on our planet. The sounds heard were the same, low, deep sounds of the universal ohm.

CHAPTER VIII

THE HOWLS, THE PATHS AND THE MISSION

The darkness created by the squall of snow and ice seemed to fall early that night, when the day was pushed far away, along with its light. Crouched inside the cave, Violet and Joaquina soon found themselves enveloped in the pitch blackness. But for the magic clothes, the narrow entrance to the cave and the fact that they were clinging to each other, the two – mainly Violet – would have gone into a state of hypothermia and died because of the loss of body temperature.

"I'm scared , Joaquina."

"That's OK!!!!!!!!!!!!!!! That's OK!!!!!!!!!!!!!

"Why is it so dark?"

"Because it's night!!!!!!!!!!!!!!!!!!"

"I'm cold."

"It'll pass!!!!!!!!!!!!! Think about the Sun and it'll pass!!!!!!!!!!!!!"

"What do you mean, think about the Sun?"

"Think about the Sun at the beach!!!!!!!!!!!!!!!!"

"Tell me a story about the Sun. Tell a warm story."

"Ah!!!!!!!!!! A Story about the Sun, no!!!!!!!!!!!!! But I'll sing for you!!!!!!!!!!!!!"

It was a lullaby very like the ones her mother used to sing. For some seconds, Violet was able to believe that she was listening to the gentle voice that would calm her almost every night, from the time she was a baby asleep in her crib. But the feeling worked like an emotional see-saw, and she was soon feeling far from home and very much alone. And solitude is as cold and dark as a cave deep in a valley. How she wished she could hear familiar voices! Instead of this, she could swear that out there she could hear the howls of snow wolves with enormous canine teeth of ice, racing and fighting with fury on the mountain sides.

Violet squeezed her eyes tight and thought: "If my daddy were here, he would see those wolves off. Yes, my daddy's strong. Those wolves would be nothing to my daddy. My daddy isn't scared of anything. Stupid wolves. My daddy's very strong. I like my daddy so much. I'd like not to be scared as well. I want my mummy. Where's my mummy? Where's my mummy's lap? Mummy, hurry up, come here, please come. Mummy, where are you?"

Joaquina went on singing quietly and then Violet remembered a time when she was only four and couldn't get to sleep, and her father told her something so comforting and unforgettable:

"Look here, I have a magic powder, and when I put it into children's eyes, they become heavy with sleep and they have a really good sleep, only waking up the next day. So be a good girl and let me put this powder in your eyes...

Since then, the imaginary powder that he pretended to rub into her eyes had become their own private trick. It always worked when Violet woke up startled in the middle of the night or couldn't get to sleep at once.

Nothing like a good emotional memory to help in difficult times. To dispel the fear and loneliness, Violet imagined that her mother was hugging her with all that affection that only mothers have, and that her father was putting the magic powder in her eyes. That was when Joaquina's lullaby put her to sleep like an animal safely tucked out of sight. Exhausted, her mind numbed and calmed, she forgot all about the snow wolves, bears and elks that the storm seemed to bring to the walls outside the cave. She heard no more. She went out like a light on the darkest, longest night of her life into a sleep so deep that, if she dreamt, she wouldn't notice and much less remember later.

Joaquina also went out like a flame in front of an open door on a cold, windy night. But she dreamt a lot. She dreamt about a world free of misery, pain and hunger. She dreamt in the way that musical notes dream, where everything is score, clefs, chord notations, pauses, point and counterpoint. She dreamt about competent, fair conductors, female and male, and happy composers. She also dreamt about consonant and dissonant chords in the middle of the symphonies of the dawns in tropical countries and also the autumn symphonies of conifer forests and the tundra lands in the northern hemisphere of the Kingdom of the Blue Earth. She finally dreamt the dreams of notes with an easy conscience.

When the first rays of sun came through the cave entrance, Violet felt something very delicate touching her face. There was a waft of air. She opened her blurry eyes and at first couldn't make out what she was seeing.

It was a butterfly the size of a thrush. It had blue and red wings; shimmering blue on the top part and hot, vibrant red at the bottom. The rest of its body was in shades of green from turquoise to the green of ferns, like those in the Atlantic Forest in the rainy season.

Its butterfly face looked a little like a human face and its voice was deep, but without so much sound power or volume. However, it was audible enough.

"Hello, and a very good morning to you! Time to wake up…"

Violet rubbed her eyes with the back of her hands, imagining that she was still asleep and dreaming.

The gentle waft of air from the flapping wings persisted.

Violet's spirit or soul then felt like a kite fluttering in the air, suddenly pulled back to the ground, where the ground was her body of flesh and the kite her spirit. She woke up, with her eyes wide. She became even prettier when she did this.

"What?"

"Good morning, beautiful morning! It's time."

Joaquina jumped and was standing upright in less than a quarter of a fast beat. She thought it was yet another enemy. But she soon came to her senses. Although she didn't judge beings by appearances, she realized at once that that vision and attitude could only be from a good being. That's because the look from that butterfly was a transparent window to its very soul.

"Good morning to you, too!!!!!!!!!!!!!! Do you want to scare me to death????????????? Do you want to give us a heart attack?"

"A heart attack, no. Get your hearts going, yes!"

"What do you mean, get our hearts going?" asked Violet. You're so pretty. Hello beautiful little butterfly."

"Get us going for what??????????? You forget that we don't have wings like you!!!!!!!!!!!!!!!! It's good that you've come to help!!!!!!!!!!!!!!!!!!!Thank you!!!!!!!!!!!! But help how??????????? We can't fly on the back of a butterfly!!!!!!!!!!!!!! One the size of you, at least. You can't imagine the tight spot we've been in up to now!!!!!!!!!!!!!!!! Get going, that's a good one!!!!!!!!!! You'd think we were going to miss the Eleven o'clock Train to Jaçana!!!!!!!!!!!!!! Can you not wait just one more minute??????????????[3] Don't be angry with her, Joaquina! She only wants to help. It's not fair. Thank you little butterfly!"

"Angry, who's angry?????????????? I'm just being practical!!!!!!!!!!!!!!! Thanks for trying!!!!!!!!!!!!!!! But if you really want to help, call someone and tell them we're stranded!!!!!!!!!!!!!!!!!!!!"

"Let's go outside. It's already here. When you least expect it, it comes...

"What do you mean, it's already here?"

"Help. It's here," said the butterfly, which rose in flight at that moment. Violet smiled wide in childlike enchantment and began to follow it to the cave opening.

"Slow down, missy in a hurry!!!!!!!!!!!!!!! Be careful !!!!!!!!! I'll go first!!!!!!!!!

It was Joaquina's turn to restrain Violet and hold her by the leg.

"Ouch!!!!!!... Okay, Madame. You go first," said the girl.

"Easy. No need to push!!!!!!!!!"

The butterfly, whose face was shining, fluttered into the outside space. A squall of wind made it suddenly gain height and it was out of sight of the two friends. It was very bright and Violet's and Joaquina's pupils were still dilated, adapted to the lack of light in the cave. Consequently, the rods

---

[3] This is a reference to the popular song *Trem das onze* by Adoniram Barbosa

and cones that are behind the eye of most living beings, connected to the ends of the optic nerves which, therefore, are light sensors, were filled with intense light. In other words, the two were temporarily blinded due to the light of day. But it only took a few seconds for the pupils to constrict and their vision to get accustomed to the light.

It was a beautiful day. Blue, cloudless sky. The blue was so vivid and the most perfect shade of indigo that only a very insensitive person would not be enthralled.

"Look, Joaquina, isn't it too much?"

Joaquina was not indifferent but she didn't have time for that natural water-colour. Her determined eyes were searching outside for the reasons why the butterfly had said what she did. When she saw it, she gave a beaming smile and exclaimed:

"Oh my, Violet!!!!!!!!!!! Look at this!!!!!!!!!!!!!!! Yippee!!!!!!!!!!!!!!!!!!!!"

A bridge of ice had formed during the night between the two stretches of interrupted trail. It was an arch of ice five metres long made from water in its solid state. Architects and civil engineers would not classify it as a Roman or Gothic arch. They would say it was a slightly arched bridge. Thus, it wouldn't put fear into anyone wanting to cross it. However, at its centre, it was very narrow. Less than forty centimetres. And there were signs that the sun rays wouldn't show it any mercy: they would soon melt it. In fact, they were already doing this at a fast pace. You could see air bubbles inside the bridge and drops of water ran from its highest point.

The bridge had been built in the middle of the storm by wolves, bears and elks, which had come to help at the behest of the liberating musical forces. These wolves, bears and elks made of diffused ice represented the wild forces of nature. They belonged to primitive sounds and music. They were the only warriors that could help in that land and in those conditions. The forces that rule wild nature had found such cowardice against a little girl and her protector unjust. They had been alerted that the two would probably be the next target of the oppressive music. So, they decided to enter the fight against the forces that wanted the end of the harmony between the wild principle of nature and the ordered world of civilisation.

"Hurrah!!!!!!!!!!!!!! It's true!!!!!!!!!!! When you most need help, it always arrives!!!!!!!!!!!!!!!!!! Never give up!!!!!!!!!!!!!!!!!!!!Hurrah!!!!!!!!!!!!!!!!!"

"Thank you dear butterfly!"

"It wasn't me. I just came to tell you. We'd better hurry. There's no time."

Joaquina went first through the mouth of the cave up to the trail. She helped Violet with the utmost care. The trail was wet with frozen snow and was like soap for any type of foot or paw.

"Crikey!!!!!!!!!!!! Go slowly!!!!!!!!!!"

"Come quickly!" begged the blue-and-red winged butterfly.

Violet dug her nails into the rock as a cat digs its claws into our clothes when it is afraid of falling from our arms.

"I'm afraid."

"Afraid of what!!!!!!!!!! I've got you!!!!!!"

Seconds later, out of breath, Violet clung to the rock wall. Her long dress covered Joaquina's face, but the note chose to say nothing so as not to run the risk of hindering the girl's descent.

"Come on!!!!!!!!!!!! Everything Ok??????????"

"Now, yes!"

"Stop the chattering. Can't you see that time is like a runaway train on a slope?," said the impatient butterfly.

"Huh! What do you mean a runaway train?" the girl shot back .

"That's enough, let's go!"

Joaquina approached the beginning of the bridge. It must have been about seventy centimetres wide. It seemed firm and solid. However, the solidity weakened as the bridge advanced over the abyss. She reflected and soon concluded that the bridge could take the weight of one them at a time. As for supporting the weight of the two, who knew? It was uncertain. It would be better to cross it one at a time. However, it would be far from responsible to allow an eight-year-old girl to do such a narrow, slippery crossing above a bottomless precipice.

"Come on. Let's go," the butterfly insisted.

"Take the belt off your dress!!!!!!!!!!!!!!!!!"

'What do you mean, take the belt off?"

"Aaaagh!!!!!! If you say 'what do you mean' once more I don't know what I'll do!!!!! Take it off now!!!!!!!!!!!!!"

Violet gave a worried frown. Then she obeyed, putting on a brave face. Joaquina slipped the belt through the buckle and wrapped it once around the child's right wrist. The other end of the belt was knotted tight around her own right leg. Bad luck that it was the distended leg.

"We're together!!!!!!!!!!!!! Come with me!!!!!!!!!!!!! Don't look down, look ahead!!!!!!!!!!!!!!! Do what I tell you!!!!!!!!!!!!!!! Together, understand????????"

Violet was afraid and looked as if she was about to cry, but she filled herself with the courage that had been increasing and growing from the beginning of that incredible journey. She controlled herself. She already knew that panic could be the most terrible of enemies.

"I'm with you, see? I'm with you! I'm with you!"

"Good girl!!!!!!!!!!!!! That's the ticket, little warrior!!!!!!!!!!!!!!!!"

They got near the bridge. The butterfly beat its wings to follow them, flying. Joaquina lay on her stomach and Violet did the same.

"This is the safest way to avoid falling!!!!!!!!!!!!! There's less pressure on the bridge like this!!!!!!!!!!!!!!

"What do..."

"Enough!!!!!!!!!!! I've already told you stop with the 'what do you mean?'!!!!!!!!!! Pay attention!!!!!!!!"

"Alright, alright. I understand. There's no need to shout. No need to be rude."

"Stop it, both of you, It's now or never!" demanded the butterfly.

They set off slowly on the crossing. First, going up the slight arch of the bridge. Violet would have closed her eyes if she hadn't been absolutely determined to overcome her fears. Centimetre by centimetre they went up and the abyss became deeper. Centimetre by centimetre the bridge became narrower. More slippery, wetter, and above all, more fragile. In this type of situation tenths of seconds seem like minutes, and seconds, hours. So they felt like the long tortuous hours marked by the clocks in medical waiting rooms.

The abyss seemed to call them to a fatal fall. Was it alive? Did it have the evil desire to
see them fall? Or was it the insecurity of someone who is not accustomed to heights? "Slowly!!!!!!!!!!!!!!!!!! That's it!!!!!!!!!!"

"I'm coming. OK."

"That's it, girls."

Having crossed exactly two and a half metres, which seemed like two and a half kilometres, they were finally at the bridge's culminating point.

"Now, it'll be easy!!!!!!!!!!!!!!!! You just need to be care!!!!!!!!!!!!!!!!"

Joaquina didn't manage to finish what she was saying. The sound of cracking ice exploded in the air. It was the most unwanted sound imaginable. A sound that should be proscribed. The highest, narrowest point of the arch could not bear the pressure per centimetre exercised by the weight of the two.

"Aaaaaaaaaaaaaaaaaaaaaaaaaaaaaaaaaaagh!!!!!!!!!!!!!!!!!!!!!!!!!!!!!"

Joaquina slid a little forwards and Violet backwards.

Below the belt that united them, the abyss began to unfold as the bridge cracked and the ice fell into the chasm's misty throat.

"Jump!!!!!!!!!!!!!"

Due to the force of gravity, Joaquina began to slip to the other side of the bridge. The belt pulled and stretched her leg and the girl's human arm. Violet, with her hand grabbing the edge of the splitting ice, and folding her legs and pressing them against the bridge, did the only sensible thing at that moment. At the end of the day, it was all or nothing. She propelled herself forwards and upwards as much as she could. She crossed through the air the short distance that separated the two sides of the broken bridge. Her propulsion was so strong, helped by the traction exercised by the belt, that her head went between Joaquina's legs, and collided with what could only be defined as the buttocks or maybe, the back of a quaver which now seemed rather like a human, now that it had two legs. The two accelerated without brakes or control in the direction of the other side of the bridge.

"Aaaaaaaaaaaaaaaaaaaaagh!"

"Hold tight!!!!!!!!!!!!!!!!!!!!!!!!!!!!!!!!!!!!!! Hold on!!!!!!!!!!!!!!!!!!"

"My God!" screamed the butterfly.

Joaquina was the first to reach the safety of the other side. Tenths of seconds later, Violet arrived. But at this crucial moment her little girl's body leaned to the side of the abyss and hung there.

"Aaaaaaaaaaaaaaaaaagh"

Foreseeing the collision, Joaquina clung to the ridges in the trail like a ship's anchor. The girl was hanging over the abyss, secured by the belt. Joaquina howled from the pain in her leg. But she wasn't the least bit worried about the pain. She merely focused on not letting go. The butterfly landed on Violet's back. She dug her feet into the girl's clothing and beat her wings with all the might her chest muscles could release.

What good did this do?

Chaos Theory is a science studied mainly by mathematicians and physicists, and sets out to explain the functioning of dynamic systems, like climate, population growth or social order movements. One of the fundaments of this theory is called "the butterfly effect," theorised in the Kingdom of the Blue Earth in 1963by the North American meteorologist, mathematician and philosopher Edward Lorenz, resulting from his studies and research carried out in The Massachusetts Institute of Technology, in the United States. The best known allegorical interpretation for this complex, advanced theory is that the beating of wings by a simple butterfly can influence the natural course of things and even cause a tornado on the other side of the planet.

But returning to the abyss where Joaquina and Violet were struggling against the force of gravity with their very lives, what good did the butterfly's attempt do? None. On the physical plane, the thrust generated by its wings did nothing against the attraction of gravity exercised on Violet. However, on the mental plane, it did make a difference. If even a butterfly would not give up on her and was playing its part, doing its utmost, then she would not be the one to throw in the towel, not her. She was a girl. And girls, like boys, can be very, very determined and strong when necessary.

We mustn't forget either that boys and girls are primates. They therefore carry an ancestral memory of more than sixteen million years of evolution, from the time when we were swinging through the trees from branch to branch on the African continent on the tiny, beautiful planet Earth. In the heart of the also called Mother Africa, our most distant ancestors, who at that time knew only wild music, also used to watch the universe with eyes wide open and feet and hands strong and agile.

Violet excelled herself. She had never trained for that. It was her ancestral primate memory that gave her instinctive wisdom. She initiated a swinging movement and, swaying slightly, she managed to grab centimetres above the rock like an experienced climber. She strained the biceps on her right arm and jumped a few more centimetres. She repeated this sequence of movements a few times.

Joaquina held on. The butterfly continued to give all it had.

"Bravo. Let's do it again!" shouted the girl, for the first time in her life playing with irony.

"Oh my dear girl!!!!!!!!!! I'll kill you!!!!!!!!!!! Come here!!!!!!!!!!!!!!!!"

The two hugged and laughed heartily. They would be friends forever. And now they had a new ally. Though fragile, the butterfly would be a very useful ally. All help was welcome.

"What's your name, lovely butterfly?"

"Pedrão"[4]

"Pedrão?"

"Pedrão?????????????????"

---

[4] Big Peter

"Why not? I'm a male butterfly. And do me a favour, don't confuse me. I came to help. But perhaps I can go now."

Joaquina and Violet held back a smile. They didn't want to offend anyone. Far less that small, lovely winged being that had been so attentive. It's just that they didn't know, nor could they, that Pedrão was a variety of the species *Danaus plexippus*, more commonly known as the monarch butterfly.

In the Kingdom of the Blue Earth, this species inhabits almost the whole of the Americas and has a more or less seven-centimetre wing span, orange with black stripes and white markings. But, in this Kingdom, the magnetism and tonalities of the seven moons made them grow and change colour.

"Thank you Pedrão. You're so beautiful, or should I say handsome. So nice. And very cute."

"Thank you very much indeed!!!!!!!!!!!!!!!!!!!! Will you be coming with us??????????????"

"It's better that way. So let's go. And don't call me cute," responded Pedrão, the butterfly, while it puffed out its monarch-butterfly chest in order to seem bigger.

"I know we have a mission. And we're going to accomplish it. Let's go and smash anyone who wants to stop us."

"Crikey!"

Girl and note looked at each other in amazement and feminine complicity. It was the first time they'd been faced with such masculine talk and energy. Joaquina started walking, not minding the pain in her leg.

Violet followed her up the mountain. Pedrão hitched a lift on the girl's shoulder. If he intended to fight, he'd better spare his energy.

The mountains now had friendly expressions and Violet didn't feel threatened by them. She walked, admiring the size and immensity of everything.

CHAPTER IX

TECTONIC FORCES AND THE PULSATION OF A KINGDOM THAT SHOULD SING

For one hour, as they were walking, Joaquina didn't look back. After all, Violet had a bodyguard now, the butterfly Pedrão. She could proceed unworried. The girl smiled constantly at the small winged being. She thought the butterfly so lovely and delicate. However, this was not how Pedrão wanted to be seen by Violet. Very much to the contrary, he had placed himself on her shoulder like a sentry on duty.

As they went further and further up, the Sun neared its zenith in the celestial dome. The sky was so clear and cloudless that at least three of the Seven Moons could be seen in the daylight. They were the Third, Fifth and Seventh Moons. The Third and Fifth were in the full-moon phase and the Seventh was waning. For this reason, the wind had the tendency to blow minor chords. If the three Moons were in the full-moon phase together, the tendency would be towards major chords. For it was the Moons that ruled the symphonies of nature by the inspiration and energy of their colours.

The chromatic variation of the light influenced and was at the same time influenced by the scales and melodies in the whole landscape.

Although the Kingdom of the Seven Moons was sad and sombre due to the devastating and painful war in its womb, it still had many wonders and melodies of happiness to inspire beings in all universes and kingdoms.

When they reached the highest point of that mountain, they felt they were on top of the world. Ice, rocks, peak after peak followed in the direction of the southwest as far as the eye could see. With one's gaze a little more to the south, a great ocean could be seen. An ocean as immense as our Pacific Ocean, and as vigorous as our Atlantic. It was no coincidence that the Kingdom of the Seven Moons had seven continents spread out equidistantly in latitude and longitude.

Violet, Joaquina and Pedrão were in the Continent of G Major. At least that's how it was written in the world maps kept in the library called the Rose Wind Universal Library, located in an incredible botanical garden, in the so-called Continent of A Major, and very well protected from the afflictions of war. It had yet to be the target of the oppressive forces of music. Almost all musical knowledge of the mineral, vegetable, animal, human and angelic evolutionary planes were recorded there on magic papyrus scrolls that could never fade, rot or be burnt. And it would be very sad to see the magic of evil wanting to corrupt them, and even though they couldn't destroy them, maybe managing to blot out the wonders recorded in them. There was knowledge that defined laws like those of some crystals that can pulsate in healing frequencies or polarise the light in luminous chords. On the same papyrus was kept almost everything about the infinite totality of music, about the pulsation of the planets, constellations, galaxies, of all the dimensions that the divine pulsation had created with its immeasurable love that sustains life.

All the planets are alive. Even those that are dying. Thus, they can be cured, despite being ill. After the intervention of the angels in the healing of its heart, the Kingdom of the Seven Moons was no longer dying and little by little its heart was returning to its tectonic singing. The continents were once again doing the eternal dance of moving the tectonic plates and the seas no longer had feverish tsunami convulsions with such frequency.

This seemed to have altered the humour of the mountains, which went back to smiling, even wanting to ease the journey of that improbable trio of butterfly, human and musical note.

But the war was from being won or ending. The oppressive forces of music were reuniting and drawing up another strategy. Though frustrated in their attempt to kill the planetary heart of the Kingdom of the Seven Moons, they still had some strategic advantages in that unhappy symphonic clash. A clash which had already generated many, many fruits of death. Violet didn't know this yet and Joaquina had not been allowed to reveal to her all the context of her epic journey, far less the ensuing risks.

Being just a girl, she really couldn't know the significance of what administrators and economists call competitive advantage, strategic planning or what the military calls tactical plans. Violet didn't know either that one of the main advantages of the forces of darkness was to torment the hope for a Better Kingdom.

For the majority of beings in the Kingdom of the Seven Moons, faith in the idea that it was worth fighting for the music of joy, health, love and elevated art had been lost. Belief in the music that brings evolution had been aborted. There was hopeless acceptance, sceptical resignation that there was nothing that could be done against the dictatorship of thought and soul.

The forces of darkness were well initiated in the science of marketing. They knew techniques on how to impose their ideas persuasively or sell subliminally. When they found it was worth it, they frequently bombarded the world with their convictions. They always claimed that it was the time to take advantage of everything, that everyone had their price, that there was no problem with corruption. For them, the ends have always justified and will always justify the means. For them there should only exist a great musical industry that would fabricate, deliver and commercialize all that was or would ever be related to the arts. This way they would have total control of the thinking and feeling of beings in all the universes. They had the same ambitions as tyrants. They yearned feverishly and compulsively for absolute power.

But, as the Kingdom of the Seven Moons should sing freely so as to inspire and feed the other universes in the kingdoms and dimensions, a girl from the Kingdom of the Blue Earth had been brought to help. Why? There was some great, unknown reason for this incredible adventure.

"Look at that mountain, it's smiling at us," said the enchanted girl.

"Mountains don't smile," responded Pedrão.

"Yes, they do. Even I can see that one there. Look, it's a giantess lying down. Can you see her face?"

"Mountains don't smile. Much less have breasts. They just let rocks fall on us."

"You have to believe it. They have life. My mother always told me that."

"Let's keep going and enough of the chatter!!!!!!!!!!!!!!!!!!!!!!! We'll soon be going down!!!!!!!!!!!!!!!!!!!!!!!"

"Pedrão, you're handsome, but it can't be like this," said Violet.

"I know that our Kingdom is upside down. Strange seasons, summers at the wrong time of year and everything else. Everyone is suffering and enslaved."

"They're difficult times indeed!!!!!!!!!!!!!!!!!!!!! But we have to proceed !!!!!!!!!!!!!!!!!!!

"I know that. Why else would I have come?" asked "the butterfly.

"So let's go," said the girl, having another one of her sudden desires to dance and twirl. "Yes, let's! But dances don't win battles. Wallops do!"

"What a fierce butterfly you are!" Violet stopped dancing and looked deep into Pedrão's eyes:

"Do we have to fight? If we're going to fight, count me out! Why can't everyone be friends? Fighting's stupid. Not nice at all."

"Violet, it's not just a fight. It's much more than that," said Pedrão.

The girl remembered the flower ball and what had happened there.

"How sad! But if that's the case, then we'll fight as well!"

"That's the ticket," shouted Pedrão. We'll turn the game around."

"Yes!!!!!!!!!!!!!!!!!!!!!!!! It doesn't matter how lost things seem to be. Lose faith, heart, never!!!!!!!!!!!!!!!!!!!!!"

"Enough of the chatter! Are we going to get walking or stay here looking at the scenery? If you're going to say here, it would be better for me to fly off alone."

They proceeded to the mountain peak. The scenery was impressive. From up there, they had a three-hundred-and-sixty degree view. It seemed they could touch the Sun. The icy peaks appeared one after the other as if the planet had a spinal column and the peaks were the vertebrae. Most of them were covered permanently in snow. They reflected the sun so much that they even blinded the eye.

Anyone looking at this trio would realize that they were different from the previous day. It was as if they were breathing in tune with the cosmos. The planet was pulsating like an instrument in a universal orchestra. And mountains are very important. They help to shape the climate, blocking and altering the movement of the clouds and the trade winds, and thus creating a cycle of rains and droughts.

The Himalayan Range in the Kingdom of the Blue Earth and the Monsoons are always coupled (and all life in India and on the Asian continent depends on this coupling), and in the Kingdom of the Seven Moons it was no different.

Scientists still have much to research to be able to place in their computer models the simulated dynamic elements that precisely define the role of the mountains in the climate game. The mountains are, in all worlds, the first link between cosmic energy and their inhabitants. The vital energy that floods the biosphere has multiple sources in the universe. Mountains also function as aerials for sources of life. Each one in its size and geometry is just like a radio antenna, tuning to a specific frequency of an energy field. This cosmic resonance with the creator is one of the links of sustenance for life.

Winds from the South blew and lifted Violet's hair, which had managed to keep its curls. Wild geese were flying approximately 10 kilometres away. They looked like white blots moving in the blue.

Violet wished she had wings and was like an eagle up high. It was as if the world were hers: she could fly over it in the blink of an eye.

Joaquina went ahead, followed by the girl and a butterfly on sentry duty. There was no sign of danger wherever they looked. Just the immensity of a world.

CHAPTER X

HEAVEN AND HELL

Meanwhile, more or less four days' journey from the top of the mountain, were two wonders as yet unknown to Violet.

One of them was a valley, with an area of more than three thousand square kilometres. It extended between two mountain chains and hills of medium height and it must have been more than fifty kilometres from one end to the other. In the centre stood an imposing castle, with seven towers reaching up a thousand metres. These same towers were interlinked by transparent tubular walkways at a height of exactly five thousand metres. The towers marked the extreme points of a seven sided polygon. Or rather, the towers were the vertices of a heptagon formed by the central body of the castle. On misty days, or when the clouds were dense and not very high, the tops of the towers could not be seen by anyone on the ground.

Since the castle's architecture formed a regular heptagon, the sum of all the interior angles was nine hundred degrees, and its sides were the same length as a thousand linear metres. Each tower was tuned to or represented one of the notes of a major musical scale. However, the distances between the towers were constant and did not obey the relations established in the musical model created by the Greek genius Pythagoras. If they had obeyed, the castle sides would have to be of a size whose relation of distance between the vertices would be the same   relative distances of the notes of a seven-note scale.

The castle also had fourteen tubular walkways at a height of one hundred and eighty metres, forming the diagonals that interlinked the seven towers. Traversing seven of these walkways were a further seven imposing towers at a height of eight hundred metres, and each tower was tuned to one of the seven musical notes

In this way, the Castle of Western Music, as it was popularly called, was formed by two heptagons: exterior and interior. It was an ingenious and unimaginable fusion of architecture and musicality, where the external towers formed major scales and the interior, minor scales.

On five of the diagonals, right at the centre of each one, there were towers of six hundred and twenty metres. They represented sustained notes or flats and were some sixty metres in diameter, while the majors measured ninety metres at the base.

One of the great magic aspects of the castle was related to the perception of anyone inside one of the towers on the vertices. This individual would see the real size of the tower they were in. However, for this observer, the heights of the other towers on the same wall would obey the same proportions followed by the musical notes of a diatonic scale of seven notes. Thus, from the perspective of the window of this first tower, the others seemed to be of a greater height. Or rather, if you entered the Tower of C, you would see the tower of B at almost double its height. The other intermediary towers also appeared to have different heights. Heights that would obey the relation of frequencies between the notes of the musical scales used in western music. However, the same lofty towers would not alter in size to those outside them.

How was this possible? What was the reason for this improbable distortion of tri-dimensional space? How to understand the relativism of the changing sizes of the towers? Would this phenomenon be an analogy of the relative difference of the passing of time for two observers at different references and different speeds, foreseen in Albert Einstein's Theory of Relativity? This is yet another magic secret of the Kingdom of the Seven Moons. The only ones who know are its architects and its Fairy Queen.

The main body of the castle was inside the interior polygon, and kept the same form of seven sides, crossed by several of the already mentioned walkways. The nave of the central hall   was the height of a one-hundred-story building. But this castle also had a party room, living rooms, sleeping quarters, guest rooms, individual bedrooms, royal apartments, halls, storerooms, concert rooms, repair workshops, carpenter's workshop, musical instrument workshop, library, audition room, museum of instruments no longer played, advanced musical research centre, small audition rooms, Winter Garden, Spring Garden, Summer Garden, Autumn Garden, basic, advanced and post-advanced music schools, multiple arts school, universal language school, engineering department, health department, greenhouse for plants of hope and so many others that it wouldn't be possible to relate them in just one story or book.

Besides the powerful magic towers, the internal gardens were stunning. Here, the seasons of the year never changed. Or in other words, the flowers, the atmosphere, the climate and even the sun seen and felt by anyone who was in the Garden of Spring were always in an eternal spring. This was the garden where the young freshness of nature and the romanticism of adolescent love were constantly present and alive in everything inhabiting the garden, in full luminosity, fragrance and energy.

In the pubescent Garden Of Spring, the pheromones were so inebriating and powerful that for short periods of time they functioned as fountains of youth for anyone who entered. This wonderful, magical effect vanished as soon as the visitor left the garden.. However, as this could be addictive to someone without the strength of spirit to enjoy this in moderation, entry into this garden was more controlled and guarded than the others.

After all, it is easy to understand this zeal. As a rock band called Queen once sang: *"Who wants to live forever.... Who dares to love forever"...* for sure all those who sang as if it were an anthem *"...I still haven't found what I'm looking for ..."* by the Irish band U2 could probably find in the Garden of Spring most of what they were looking for. A place bursting with the most exotic, unknown and beautiful flowers, embellished by the songs of birds and cicadas.

The same logic went for the other gardens, like Summer, where the afternoons were as hot and humid as a tropical forest. No other garden pulsated as intensely in the life and birth of species as the summer garden. There, the days were long and sun-drenched and the rains fell at six in the evening on the dot in refreshing, heavy showers. In this garden, the midday sun actually burnt. However, it was the ideal, most delicious place to bathe in a waterfall or splash with the foamy waves of the South Seas. In the Garden of Summer, life was at its peak of fertility and sexual vigour.

In the Garden of Autumn, the light reflected in the leaves and flowers, many of which prepare to wither and be reborn in spring, resembled the paintings by the Impressionists of the Kingdom of the Blue Earth: Van Gogh, Monet, Renoir and so many others.

It was filled with red and yellow flame trees. On some occasions, this garden exhaled the fragrances of nostalgia. On others, depending on the time of day, the scenario was even more beautiful and passionate than all the other gardens. That was because it brought the experience of life, and did not see it as a prelude to the end of a symphony, but as a flame that must always be celebrated.

This was the garden of the flowers that are their own masters. It was the garden of flowers that had already lived juvenile romanticism, the fire of adolescence, the fulfilling vigour of adult life, and now savoured everything deeply and calmly. It was the garden of the flowers and plants which were no longer the victims of illusions or siren songs, but which had the hope and experience to be happy and continue their missions.

It could be supposed that the Garden of Winter was the Garden of old plants. But this would be a fatal error of observation. Here, snow covered almost the entire ground. The preponderance of trees was pines, araucarias and many conifer species. But it did have flowers in quantity and impressive diversity for such a cold place. It was not the garden of old, withered or dead flowers. It was a garden of seeds that would sprout in the eternal cycle of life. The flowers that withered became seeds to be born in the Garden of Spring. It was the garden of plants and flowers happy at seeing their missions accomplished, which waited for a new cycle.

But what area did the four gardens occupy inside the castle? The reply isn't so simple. What's certain is that they were immense, though finite. In them, even a hummingbird could fly in a straight line for days until it reached a transparent crystal wall opposite the great diamond front door. This was only possible because the engineering and magic, far more advanced than the most advanced technologies or magic, were ruled by two groups of laws of physics and metaphysics.

In other words, from the outside, the walls, towers and battlements occupied space and functioned inside the perceptible principle for many beings as a tri-dimensional space. Inside the Castle of Music, the time dimension, the gravitational field dimension, the vibratory frequency dimension and the dimension of the imagination moulded and commanded space, making everything solid dissolve in the air and recompose according to its shape, time, sequence and necessary order.

There is no other work in the universe of humans, known or unknown, that would dare to compete with it.

Nor are there any other spring, summer, autumn or winter gardens so passionate, symbolic and magic. It is believed that it was the Gardens of the Castle of Music that inspired the music of the Italian composer Antonio Vivaldi, in1723, to compose one of his masterpieces, the four concertos for violin and orchestra "The Four Seasons".

The Castle of Western Music was very well protected. Its battlements included exterior towers and formed the seven vertices.

They were also very high. Almost two hundred metres separated the turrets from the green carpet of the valley. Their solidity and resistance had almost no limits. They were made from a mixture of gold, titanium, diamonds and a metal unknown to us, much heavier than lead. Its composition also included carbon fibre and magic polymers. This mixture was developed inside a solar forge that only magic before the beginning of time knew.

Whoever executed this wonderful chemical metallurgy no longer moved in any known dimension. It had been a special gift for the Fairy Queen of Music. Thus, the battlements were indestructible by the action of time, explosion or collision of any projectile.

However, as with everything, it had weak a spot. Its molecular, atomic, and subatomic structure was put together in crystals of the highest vibration. So, the frequency of the sad, enslaved and treacherous notes, if they were in very great quantity and intensity and in the right tone, could damage them.

As a very imprecise analogy, just as with the Walls of Jericho, only music could defeat them. And it was because of this that the oppressive forces of music were working arduously, with their best "maestros" and scientists. They believed they had the answers and were preparing the cruellest attack on this target.

In the Castle vale ran two rivers born in distant hills. One was called the River of the Stones of Voices and the other was the River of the Mermaids. The River of Voices emptied into the River of Mermaids, after partially circumnavigating the castle. It was this river that supplied the castle with precious water.

There were enormous concave mirrors and tubes forming a great organ of optic fibres in the distant hills, which reflected and balanced the energy received by the seven sides of the Castle.

This entire story was taking place in the southern Hemisphere of the planet and the side called The Castle's Sun Tower was the one that faced the North Pole. As this side was, therefore, the north side, it used to receive much more solar and lunar energy than the others.

But the Castle of Music had been conceived to be one hundred per cent balanced in everything. An ingenious system of reflection and polarization of the solar light and magnetism of the seven Moons, which was in the hills, was automatically adjusted by the magic of the balance to compensate for the different energy fluxes occurring on each side

We must also add that the Castle of Western Music was, in every sense, perfectly sustainable. It had light, wind and magnetism catchers. Its walls were covered by a film adapted for the conversion, use and distribution of the diverse forms of energy mentioned. It also recycled all the water consumed and made use of the rains. No sewage, rubbish or any solid residue was disposed of in any part of the Kingdom of the Seven Moons because its cellars housed several clean rooms for advanced recycling.

The environmental impact on the valley was zero. A paradise for those who wished to learn such sciences as Sustainable Food Production, Global Sustainability, Biochips, Intelligent Polymers, Astrophysics and Solar Metallurgy Applied to Sciences of Organic and Inorganic Materials, Nanotechnology and an ancient, occult science of the Kingdom of the Blue Earth called Nanomagic of Clean Life Materials.

The Castle was everything that is good for lovers of music, arts and sciences. However, it was not so easy to get permission to visit it, study or work there. Only because of great merit and on special occasions did its enormous, indestructible gates open to those happy ones admitted. There, the political and social regime was the most advanced meritocracy that can be imagined and so the vale and its surroundings would always be preserved.

But it was not this happy scenario which reigned at that moment. An enormous dark, stinking stain was advancing from the north. At first it was far away, born where the leafy vegetation met a desert region that hadn't existed two hundred years before Violet became part of this story.

One day what had existed there was a beautiful, majestic forest of oaks, baobabs and Brazil wood. It was the wilful and indiscriminate use of large tree and flower clamping and cutting machines that had caused the great desertification and prepared the way.

But if the desert of earth sick with erosion was recent, the dark stain was even more so. Little by little, the stain advanced, chewing, spitting, swallowing and even vomiting everything that was good and alive. They were the same bubbles of foetid pitch used in the battle at the flower ball. As there is no rest for the wicked, the bubbles had been improved as weapons of sadness and death. Now they had an osmotic hunger and a borrowed subconscious desire to spoil everything.

Launched by the same catapults operated by an infantry of baboons, men and women with strange expressions, this time they were countless in number. Seen from above, they looked like an army of carnivorous ants: army ants or driver ants.

They advanced, marching in double time, the strong beat always marked by the left legs of the men, women and baboons. This army was marching slowly and with determination in order to disguise the individual cowardice of the combatants. From time to time, a sound echoed, in the style of pile driver electronic music, an ode to idleness and pornography, full of sonic and subsonic noises. The army was thus unsettled and in desperation began to smell and sniff with their noses in the air. This was when enormous shining trumpets sprayed *coorraína* into the air.

The army of the oppressive forces of music occupied an area of almost five hundred square kilometres, with many steam pianolas. They were even bigger than the pianola seen by Violet at the beginning of her adventure. But one, much smaller, was scarier than all the others. Captain of the pianola platoon, this smaller one had developed intelligence and malign feelings.

They were smoking and burning the wood from many of the old trees that had been there before the desertification. It was even possible to hear the old screams of pain in the crackling of the burning wood. But the pianolas and the enslaved and already converted notes just cackled. The generals and other high-ranking officers, just like the pianolas, used filter masks so as not to inhale the *coorraína*. They needed to stay lucid to observe, decide on strategy and command their divisions, near-zombies from brain and soul washing.

The arsenal of this macabre army also included hundreds of different instruments of various sizes, preceded by four hundred sand-coloured worms the size of hump-backed whales.

They would be used as living machines to dig tunnels underneath the castle walls. These same creatures produced thick slime, sticky and acidic, which protected them against attacks: from bee stings to the claws of a polar bear. As this acid didn't go very well with pitch, they marched ahead of the army, and wherever they passed, they left a wretched cloud of sulphurous vapour, emitting a smell that put an end to grass, vegetation and any living thing.

They were called the Worms of the Obsessive Stickiness of Envy. A terrible mutation developed in the incubating laboratories of the oppressive forces of music, a type of sandworm common in nature. Fruit of a cross between various generations of selected worms, they were created by scientists who used genetic engineering techniques and hybrid stem cells. This race was fed spiritually by the worst tacky music, destined to foment envy and sick passions and jealousies. They became very powerful weapons of war. But in limited numbers. Their creation had been interrupted because they had an insatiable hunger and would only stop growing when they self-exploded.

They had become a huge problem even for the Forces of Oppressive Music. Any carelessness and they could devour soldier, notes and generals.

As there were not enough supplies for them, the oppressive forces themselves feared them. To calm them, they promised that inside the Castle of Music energy and food would be infinite. The Forces of Oppressive Music celebrated the fact that the Worms of Obsessive Stickiness had believed them and began their campaign as quickly as they could so as to use that huge headache in their favour.

The air force of the oppressors had not yet appeared, but the Worms advanced, followed by the dark stain and the macabre legions. They advanced and when they could not bear the hunger, they were fed enslaved notes – especially when, exhausted, they did not have the strength to proceed. Now and again, their long, sticky tongues also managed to grab one baboon or another, their favourite food.

CHAPTER XI

FAME AND THE DREAMS OF THE RATS

The immensity of the world. It was this thought that inspired Violet, perched on the edge of a rock wall that formed the most spectacular precipice recorded in any geographic atlas. It fell some two thousand metres vertically until it hit a rocky projection, where the trail began again. Violet felt a chill run down her spine, but even so she continued to drink in the views of the immensity with her lively eyes.

This was when she looked more to the east and noticed the Green Valley and the river of Voices and River of Mermaids. She could see, almost at the limit of what could be made out, the Castle of the Seven Towers or the Castle of Western Music. As the attack by the Oppressive Forces was coming from the north side of the Castle, she didn't notice the dark morning that was appearing at the north limit of the valley, advancing at the slow speed of the giant worms.

"How lovely...Is that a castle?"

"It's much more than that!!!!!!!!!!!!!!!!!!!! It's our reason for living!!!!!!!!!!!!!!!"

"It's the home and power of our queen," replied Pedrão, with the face of a very stubborn butterfly. He kept on puffing out his chest.

"They want to finish it off. But I won't let them."

"What do you mean they wa..............?"

She didn't manage to end the sentence because Joaquina cut her short.

"I've already said that I can't take any more of your 'What do you mean?' young lady.!!!!!!!!!!!!!!!!!! Don't take any notice of this butterfly!!!!!!!!!!!!!!!!!!!!!! A long walk awaits us !!!!!!!!!!!!!!!!!!! And there's no walk without a walker!!!!!!!!!!!!!!!!!!!!!!!! And if there's no walker, there's no walk either!!!!!!!!! And then, it no longer awaits us!!!!!!!!!!!!!!!!!! Let's go while it's still there waiting!!!!!!!!!!!!!!!!!!! Aha!!!!!!!!!!!!!! Aha!!!!!!!!!!!!!!! Aha!!!!!!!!!!!!!!! That was a good one!!!!!!!!!!!!!!!!!!!!!! Ahhhhhhhh!!!!!!!!!!!!!!!!!!!!!!!!!! And no more of the 'What do you mean?'!!!!!!!!!!!"

Pedrão waggled his head and stuck out his chest again. Violet, for her part, looked at Joaquina with a doubtful expression, only to smile immediately afterwards.

"I see! Why make it wait, if it doesn't know how to wait? Very good!"

"That's all we need. A note that's a show-off and practical joker and a girl who thinks she knows about philosophy. Enough of the chatter. Let's get going," said the butterfly.

"Cool! Are we going to the Castle? Who lives there?"

"No! We're going somewhere else!!!!!!!!!!!!!! Maybe you'll be lucky!!!!!!!! Maybe with the blessings of the heavens and the Moons you'll be able to see it one day????????????????"

"Perhaps one of us could see it and even go in there again?" concluded Pedrão. At that moment the girl's expression changed like the wind. It was a streak of sadness mixed with frustration.

"Why not? Isn't it fair? It's so lovely. And what's that black smoke? Look, it's making a cloud. What's that?"

"So it's begun," said Pedrão, frowning.

"Yes, it has indeed!!!!!!!!!!!! And we're late!!!!!!!!!!!!!!!!!!!!!"

"I've already said that there's too much chatter and not enough action."

"So, what are we waiting for????????????? Let's go!!!!!!!!!!!!!!"

"Hold on, guys, what's begun?"

'Let's get going, darling!!!!!!!!!!!!!!!!!!! I'll tell you later!!!!!!!!!!!!!!!!!"

"Later, always later."

Joaquina looked at Violet with tenderness and apprehension. Doubts about the impact of the pressures and challenges on that eight-year-old girl brought back lines to her musical face. She would not give up because she was faithful to her very important mission, a mission she was never sure she deserved or was able to accomplish. She had never been certain either about the reason for that mission. Her only conviction was that, if necessary, she would give her own life for the girl or for the Kingdom of the Seven Moons that she loved so much.

She looked again at her task force and saw an ingenuous child beside a butterfly who was speaking like a stocky security guard or an MMA fighter.

"Come here, darling. Let's go down anchored to each other!!!!!!!!!!!!!!!!!"

"Anchored?"

"Take off your belt!!!!!!!!!!!!!!!!!!!!!!!!!!!"

"I know, as we did at the ice bridge. Ah ha! I'm smart, see?"

"Ok. From now on all the care in the world won't be enough. It's going to be tiring and don't look down!!!!!!!!!!!!!!!!!!!!!"

"Of course I'll look down. I'm smart."

"Chatter. Chatter. Too much chatter."

"I know, and not enough action!!!!!!!!!!!!!!!!!!!"

"Very funny."

Seconds later the girl's right wrist was joined by the belt to the improbable leg of a quaver. Marching backwards and with four supports, Violet was nearing the abyss. Pedrão was moving clinging to the cloth at the back of her dress.

Joaquina imitated her and together they went down, foot before foot. It could be seen that the gradual metamorphosis of Joaquina had left her reasonably anthropomorphic and thus, besides two legs, she now had two arms and two hands.

"Let's go like this. A little more to the right with the leg. More! No not like that! Come back. Come back!" was the command bellowed by Pedrão seconds before everything would be lost.

"Ahhhhhhh!"

A loose rock slid from the top of the mountain and they saw it no more. Happily, what plummeted was the rock and not Violet, who almost took a wrong step right at the beginning of the almost endless descent.

"Let's try again."

"Make sure you guide the girl better!!!!!!!!!!!!!!!!!!!!!I can't see from here!!!!!!!!!!!!!!!"

"But you don't need to be a blind anchor."

"Stop fighting. If there's going to be fighting, count me out. You're an irritating pair."

"Slowly. Slowly. Right foot just a little over there."

"Over there, where?"

"To the right. That's it. That's it. Your first foot's already gone. Now it's the left foot. That's it. No. No! Now go. Go down one step with your right foot. Grab the step with your hand. Go down a little with the other foot. That's it. That's right. Come on. Let's go. Both hands holding tight. That's it!"

"Hurrah! This is too much!"

It was the shout from the girl that resonated and echoed through the precipices and mountains. Violet saw herself on a kind of ladder formed by steel bars embedded in the solid rock. There were three thousand of these bars bent into the shape of seventy-centimetre staples, twenty-five centimetres deep, of which five were stuck into the mountain. The face of the most solid rock was ridged and cold. Some staples, or steel steps, were rusty or twisted. The average distance between the steps was twenty-eight centimetres and fifty seven millimetres, an extreme ladder. But this wasn't the reason for Violet's vertigo. She screamed with euphoria through feeling like the bravest high-altitude mountain climber. They were ten thousand metres up. How could a girl breathe in this condition of such rarefied air and not freeze. This was yet another work by the magic that governed that Kingdom.

"Bravo! Hurrah!" she roared once again.

In reply to Violet's shouts, they heard the powerful screeching call of a peregrine falcon that glided practically stopped in mid-air, four thousand metres up, on the lookout for some careless rat for lunch.

"But, what a girl!!!!!!!!!!!!!!!!!!!!!!!!! Let's go carefully!!!!!!!!!!!!!! And you be careful, too, Pedrão!!!!!!!!!!!!!!!!! A gust of wind might catch you unawares!!!!!!!!!!! Your face will be squashed against the rock face!!!!!!!!!!!!!!"

"Keep walking funny girl. There's too much talking. Walk two together, go on."

They began the two-thousand-metre descent. Violet was enjoying it. This time her fears didn't show. Who can understand girls?

They pressed on, step by step. In Violet's view everything continued
to be spectacular
and this was the best part of the adventure. She'd tell everyone at school about that descent.

"Pity there's nobody filming. I'd love to show this at school."

"Who says we're here to produce film stars?"

"Pedrão!!!!!!!!!!!!!!!! She's just a girl !!!!!!!!!!!!!!! Let her dream!!!!!!!!!!!!!!!!!!"

"I know, I know, he's going to say "too much chatter". Do you see? You're the most beautiful and also the most bad-tempered little butterfly that exists."

Pedrão was going to a react to Violet's last observation and say:

"Little butterfly indeed. I'm big."

But he decided to stay quiet and clung on tighter to the flowery material of the girl's dress. The wind was gaining force as the day got shorter and the light dimmed. It was getting hard to stay still, and because butterflies can't fold their wings, they always receive the full force of the wind. Two and a half hours later they were at the eight thousand metre mark. The wind was bringing the cold with it and hurrying on the arrival of night. The steps had ended and the trail reappeared on the rocky plateau where they were standing. Soon they arrived at another fork. Violet was following Joaquina, who had taken the opposite direction to the Castle of Western Music. The way was easy without many cracks in the rocks and so the descent accelerated their steps.

On the other hand, the wind didn't let up. Much to the contrary: it was cold, cold enough to bring tears to the eyes of anyone there. It was Pedrão who was suffering the most. Butterflies are like many sailors. They like breezes, light and strong winds, but they can't bear gusts of uncontrolled whirlwinds.

"Phew, we're where I wanted us to be. We'll be taking shelter here!!!!!!!!!!!!!!!! Now that it's dark, it's more dangerous!!!!!!!!!!!!!!!!!!"

They were three thousand five hundred metres down and had covered twenty kilometres of winding, beautiful trail, with no great dangers. The vegetation had returned to the landscape and was typical of such altitudes. Five of the Seven Moons were shining in the sky. The other two still hadn't risen for those at that latitude and longitude of the planet. Even so, the night remained dark because of the lunar eclipse of the Fourth moon and mainly because of the heavy rain clouds that, pushed and shoved by the wind, appeared during the last hours of the walk. Many of them complained when they crashed into each other, releasing thunder and lightning.

Insect, musical note and human went into the cave already known by the musical note. It soon began to rain. The mischievous wind spat the moisture of the rain onto the expeditionary force of three. Pedrão hated it because of this: his wings were in wretched condition because of the cold and damp. Violet, for her part, imagined what the wind was going to do to her frizzy hair. This was what she had read one day in a fashion and beauty magazine. It's just that she didn't really know what frizzy hair was. But this didn't matter now. She was starting to feel peckish. She'd spent much more energy than even the magic of the food offered by the arum lily could supply. And in times of 'peckish', 'hungry' or 'famished', vanity always gets pushed to the background, especially for a child.

Tired, the girl and musical note went to sleep in each other's arms. Pedrão stayed on guard duty at the cave entrance and from time to time vented his butterfly complaints to the wind.

Lightning and thunder came one after the other in the clash of clouds. The rain was torrential, Violet's discomfort, too. She couldn't find a position comfortable for her back on that hard floor, where small rivulets of water were running to the back of the cave. She got up. Joaquina was snoring. Snoring? This was really bothering her. Pedrão was asleep in his sentry position. Flashes of lightning entered the cave and projected the shadow of a winged being with the soul of a fighter in the skin of a butterfly. The image of the shadow was more in keeping with his spirit than his real appearance.

Violet's dress was damp at the hem and this bothered her. In a temper, she squatted down near the entrance.

"Is this rain ever going to stop? What a horrid cave? I think there are slimy lizards in here. I don't like it here. It's so ugly," she thought. Her bad humour increased, along with her despondency.

It wasn't the next flashes of light that caught the girl's attention, but the reflections of sparkling silver and gold light hitting her forehead and eyes. They were coming from the middle of the forest and the more silvery and golden they became, the worse the girl's spirits and discomfort grew.

She looked at Pedrão, who now looked to her like a very ugly, irritating butterfly.
All he talked about was "chattering" and "Let's get going". But what was really annoying was that musical note who thought she was human. She wanted to go back home. Would it be good to go home without seeing the rest? Without seeing the Castle? How she wanted to be the princess of the castle...

The moment the wind and rain let up, the reflections grew and brought intoxicating, low music, inside the cave. The aroma of popcorn with butter invaded the space, along with the smell of hamburgers ready to be devoured. It was an assault on her little nose. The music acted like a sleeping draught on Joaquina and Pedrão, but for Violet it was hypnotising.

From the middle of the forest, where the reflections were coming from, she saw an unusual cortège. In two lines, rats the size of pit bulls were marching in four-four time. They were red and very hairy, smiling, showing strong rodent teeth. Their looks were penetrating, but hid their souls from anyone looking at them. The four rats in the fourth column on the left and the other four in the column on the right formed the front line of the troop. In the centre of the two columns of rodents were two large, circular beds with blood red satin lining the base. They were made up with Egyptian cotton sheets and fluffy pillows. Each one was being carried by one hundred and fifty rats of normal size, though very muscular. And believe it or not: they were all bathed and perfumed with the best of what the perfume industry can produce.

One of the beds had a kind of TV with a one hundred-and-eighty-two-inch flat screen, only four millimetres thin, attached to the headboard. The reflections seen on some parts of Violet's journey, and also now, had their origin in this television from the other world.

The woman lying down the second bed was more than astonishing. Blonde, red-head, brown-skinned, black, Asian or indigenous, she satisfied with her different types the taste of anyone who desired her. Curvaceous and long and lean at the same time, she had voluptuous breasts sculpted by a bikini made of pink and violet purpurin. She was also wearing semi-transparent, flowing harem pants, like those worn by belly dancers.

She had such a beautiful, perfect face that it could only belong to a good person. By her side, a silver tray, encrusted with rubies and diamonds, held a decorated silver bucket where a bottle of the best champagne was chilling, along with a can of diet soda. On the first bed, with the TV, there was also a tray full of fresh strawberries covered in delicious dark chocolate under a layer of sweet white chocolate. They triggered an irresistible desire to bite into them. Beside the tray there was another one with hamburgers and industrialised french fries.

The reflections and lights emitted by the TV showed distorted images at first. But, little by little, Violet started to recognise them. In a possible future, she was looking at herself as a pop star.

"Come here, princess of the Kingdom of the Blue Earth," was what Violet heard.   "Princess, me? What an amazing voice that woman has. My goodness, how beautiful she is. I'd love to be like that," thought the girl, for the first time with a different kind of smile on her child's face. It sketched on her, indelibly, an adolescent smile.

'Come, my friend. Enough of suffering. It's time to shine. You deserve it. You didn't ask to be born in your world, far less in this one. So, since you were born there and here, you deserve it. You deserve everything that's good! Don't you agree?"

When they met, the hunger and the aroma of food stuck together like shoemaker's glue. Violet's mouth was watering, while her spirit was penetrated by the "futile pride vanity type A negative".

A moment when time was the only thing moving in the forest. Everything else had come to a halt, waiting to see what a fascinated, dreamer Violet would do. Then she looked back. Joaquina and Pedrão were out for the count. It was the effect of the tiredness allied to the music that sounded to them like music played by snake charmers.

"Can I have a hamburger and then four chocolates?"

"Of course, they're yours. You deserve them, after everything you've been through. And there's more.

I know that since you began to study the piano you've wanted to play to the world. You have a brightness in your soul. I will make you famous. I can do this because I have the power. And the desire to do it."

"Famous, me, ? Like the girl fro..."

Violet had no time to finish what she was saying. The woman laughed out loud: "Far more than her. How many like her have I made? I didn't make them all famous, but I did make a lot of them so. Far more than my, let's say, my old rival."

"What do you mean by I didn't make all of them and I made a lot of them?"

"Ah, that's of no interest!"

The stunning woman changed her voice and facial expression subtly. A second later she went back to normal.

"My dear, I am the Fairy Queen of Fame. I'll make you famous, a real celebrity. Look. Look at yourself in action."

The sound was intense. Many instruments playing a fusion of styles: pop, rock, "world music" and Latino rock resounded magisterially. Perfect arrangements and dance music.

On the screen, Violet could see herself. She had become a pop star among pop stars. She was the most popular girl in school. Rich, very rich. Whenever she left her house, at least ten bodyguards in suits and dark glasses cleared the way for her. At the door of her shows a legion of fans screamed her name:

"Violet, Violet, we want Violet!"

She saw herself so powerful and famous that she had even stopped her piano lessons. After all, the world was already affirming that she was great. No more boring, long, tiring exercises. From here on, just fun and more fun. She could buy everything for herself, her parents, her grandparents. Thinking about her parents, she noticed that she couldn't see them properly on the screen. Deep inside, she knew they still loved her. That much was certain. But for the Violet in the TV images, they were distant. It was to her impresarios that she spoke most. She also had a name and brands and more brands of dolls, beauty products and must-have designer clothes. In that probable future time was money, fame and glamour. The Violet of the future was beautiful, with a fantastic body. In her video clips, she played, sang and danced sexily, dressed in the most famous designer clothes and shoes in the world. In the world that lay at Violet's feet, Violet at fifteen years of age.

"Is that what I'll be like when I'm fifteen? Is it possible to be so famous?"

"My dear, that's nothing. That's just the trailer."

"But where are my mother and father?"

"And who cares about them? You should be thinking about what you want, be more focussed."

"*I* care about them!"

"Good girl! That's exactly what I wanted to hear from your mouth. You've passed the selfishness test. I didn't show you your parents just to see if you really were nice. They'll be fine, I guarantee it."

"What do you mean by "I guarantee it"?

The rats looked at each other, smiling maliciously. That was when Pedrão woke up from his deep sleep and, without making a sound, went over to nudge Joaquina. He covered the note's mouth with one of his wings:

"Quiet, we can't be too careful. We have to surprise them all at once. On my signal, you get the girl, and I'll fly into the witch's eyes."

"What witch????????? The sounds escaped from the mouth of the still sleepy note.

It was enough for the Fairy Queen of Fame to notice. But she didn't show any reaction perceptible to the inattentive. A slightly raised right eyebrow gave the order for four bats the size of ladybirds to enter the cave and bite the note and butterfly in the jugular vein. As Pedrão and Joaquina were not fully awake, they didn't react and went back to sleep. The minute flying rats were the feared, wretched vampire bats that feed on the vital fluid of their victim. In a short time, Joaquina and Pedrão would be good for nothing, then they would die in agony. Violet noticed nothing. However, if her reasoning trusted the Fairy, her instinct didn't.

"But what will I have to do?"

"Nothing, Or almost nothing. Just two little things of minimal importance. First, want me as your companion, and say goodbye to those two bores you've been going around with. Then, swear that you'll play what I ask you to play."

"Swear? What if I don't like the music?"

"OK. You don't need to swear, just promise."

"Promise"?

"Alright. Alright. Just say out loud that you'll listen and think. There's no harm in that. Is there? You're a smart girl. You're very intelligent and nobody's fool. This is the kind of girl I admire."

At that moment, a memory came back to her. She recalled one of the many times that she'd been walking in the Mantiqueira Range. She could smell the Atlantic Forest in the mountains that separate the states of São Paulo, Rio de Janeiro and Minas Gerais. Then she remembered that her father had said that parents must, among other things, teach their children good values because one day they would be responsible for themselves and would have to make their own decisions. She recalled that her mother had always told her to be true to her friends and that a shooting star shines very bright, but not for long.

"So, my friend. Embrace fame and lie on the bed. These are the sweetest sweets in the world. Try one, just one. What harm is there in trying just one?"

Violet smiled. So did the Fairy. The girl's eyes sparkled, the Fairy's big eyes even more so. Violet saw everything very clearly. She finally understood what her mother and father had wanted to teach her.

"Can I lie down a little with you? Will I be pretty like you?"

"Even more so, my love. Come"

On the Fairy's command, the army of rats made a ladder of flesh, fur and tails. Violet gently placed her little feet, clad in the magic freebie ballet slippers, on the rat-ladder. The rats made a noise, but they easily bore the girl's weight. Step by step she went up, until she reached the bed.

"Can I have what you're drinking?"

"Dear girl, this is not for a child. Take the soft drink, it's diet. It doesn't make you fat."

Violet pouted. Looking disappointed.

"But, on second thoughts, a half a glass won't do any harm. Just half a glass!"

Violet smiled. She bent over slightly and took the champagne from the ice bucket, standing it upright on the cloth. She made to take one of the glasses and, suddenly, she banged like thunder with both hands under the tray. With her all her might she threw the tray with ice bucket and all against the Fairy's face.

"You witch! Do you think I'd leave my friends to your rats? Pedrão, Joaquina, wake up! Help!"

The act was so unexpected and the water in the bucket so cold that it clouded the Fairy's eyes at the very instant she fell backwards. To increase her fury further, the bucket handle gave her a superficial cut on the left cheekbone. Violet lost no time, and grabbed the champagne. She went down the rat ladder, light and agile, as at the beginning of break time at school, when she used to race the boys to see who'd get to the cafeteria first. She poured champagne on them and they dispersed, sticky and squealing.

The girl ran screaming. The body-guard rats decided to help their queen. However, one went after her and all the rat found was a hard bottle thrown in its direction. That was some whack. It must have really hurt, because it smashed on the rat's forehead and caused a bump that would never heal. Though in pain, the rat tried to grab the girl's dress by the hem with its teeth. The confusion and screaming distracted the bats inside the cave. Joaquina and Pedrão woke up

.

"What's happening???????????? What's happening????????????"

"Fight! It's a fight! Where?"

"Run!" yelled Violet.

The three bolted to the trail below like Olympic cyclists. Violet and Joaquina, propelled by their legs, and Pedrão by a fine pair of wings. In three agonizing seconds, they'd covered thirty metres.

"Wretches!! Damn girl! Get them! I want to make juice from their kidneys and livers! If I don't get theirs, I'll have yours!"

Anyone who had heard the Fairy Queen of Fame's voice at first would never, even being tortured and interrogated, say it was the same voice now. Not even the worst of the worst witches would have emitted a voice in such a heinous tone. Her subordinates careered after the fugitives in desperation. After all, it was their own kidneys and liver at stake.

Violet and Joaquina were running, beating every record for human speed. They were going at forty-five kilometres an hour. Small rats were no match for them. But the big ones caught up at the fifty-kilometre mark and, snarling and showing their strong rodent teeth, were gaining ground. It was just a question of time.

Violet looked back. She saw the trail getting further away and the rats approaching.

"Ahhhhhhhhhh! Run!"

"Faster!!!!!!!!!!!!!!!! Faster!!!!!!!!!!!!!!!!!!!"

Pedrão would have had no problem escaping by flying, but he was flying over the heads of the other two. He soon realised that the initial advantage of thirty metres was now less than twenty. So he decided to stop his flight and face the large rodents. Poor thing, he wouldn't stand the least chance.

A clash unfolded between giant rodents, scared by the moods of their Queen, against the butterfly who thought he was good in a fight. Joaquina and Violet pushed forward, until the girl looked back:

"Joaquina, stop!"

"What now???????????"

"Look! We have to help!"

"But that butterfly's crazy!!!!!!!!!!!!!!!!!!!!!!! And clueless!!!!!!!!!!!!!"

Rats and butterfly were less than three metres apart. For Violet and Joaquina time passed like a film shot at a thousand frames a second and then played back at normal speed. They could see the impact slowly and in minute detail. When there were just exactly one hundred centimetres to the end of that butterfly's body's existence, seven white-winged stallions came careering down the mountain slopes and trampled the big rats sideways. There was almost nobody left to tell the story. Six rats fell against the slope and two managed to halt before the collision. The displacement of air provoked by the horses had a contrary "butterfly effect" on Pedrão. He started spinning in the whirlwind of the semi-vacuum that had been caused, and fell on his back against a giant tree leaf. He was knocked unconscious but soon came round at the hands of Violet, who had come back with Joaquina to rescue him. Spurred on by the fear imposed by the Fairy Queen of Fame, the two surviving rats plucked up, who knows from where, the courage to face the horses. They stood on their hind legs and snarled in a position of attack. To no avail. They ended up being trampled to death.

A beautiful woman could be seen mounted on the biggest horse. She was dressed in the most discreet way possible. However, she had a fascinating, uncloying beauty. The Amazon then declared in a friendly voice:

"Run. Keep going. I'll deal with her, leave it to me."

Mouth gaping open in fascination, Violet turned to Joaquina and asked:

'Who's she?"

"Don't be so curious, I'll tell you later!!!!!!!!!!!!!"

"Later! Later! It's always the same. For children, if it's fun everything's always later. But when it's time to be told off, everything's now."

"Joaquina, even though it's chatter, she's right," Pedrão observed. Violet turned to the woman with the white winged horses:

"Lady. Hey, lady. Please, Madame."

The Amazon saviour looked back while her horses grouped again.

"Thank you very much. You saved my friend, and us."

'I'm the one who's grateful and proud, Violet. Keep going ahead. There's no time to lose. The great battle has begun. Rest assured that I'll deal with all the pretence. That phoney owes me big time."

Obeying without question, Violet, Joaquina and Pedrão began their march again, taking long strides. Then the girl gave Joaquina an order.

"Don't even think about saying "later". Who is she?"

"The Fairy Queen of Real Fame. She's the Fairy of True Fame. The fame of those who deserve it for their merits and deeds.

"I understand."

"How do you mean 'understand', just like that ????????????? Aren't you going ask "what do you mean for their merits and deeds?"

"No. I understand and that's it."

The Fairy Queen of Real Fame went back up the trail to face her arch-enemy, who had had enough time to call more rat slaves.

"You bitch. You were only supposed to test her, not seduce her with promises."

The Fairy Queen of Fame and enslaved rats feigned indifference. The other continued her tirade:

"Irresponsible, you were even going to let her drink. Did it have *coorraína* in it? Did it? Answer me! Don't look as if you know nothing about it.

"Maybe yes. Maybe no. But the one who went back on their word is you. Incidentally, my friend, you owe me lots of rats."

"And you still had the nerve to pursue her! Witch! To pursue a child!"

The Fairy Queen of Easy Fame's mask fell suddenly and her voice exploded:

"Square! Frigid. Sexless cow!"

"You really have no class at all"

"Get out of my way! I'm going to get that wanna-be pop star. She's mine. Only mine. And as for you my lady of good manners, it would be good, very good, if you provided me with a lot of rats."

"Try to get past me, then. Come on!"

The Fairy Queen of Real Fame then intoned some of her most beautiful songs. The other counter attacked with thousands of her famous vulgar, banal songs. The tunes clashed against each other in the air several times. For Violet, Joaquina and Pedrão, already far away, these collisions looked like new flashes of lightning tearing and lighting up the skies terrifyingly.

In the end, on the battle field of fame, the thousands of fabricated tunes were no match for the music of the Fairy Queen of Real Fame. The wrinkled Fairy Queen of Easy Fame, her hair dishevelled, could no longer continue the battle. Her superficial beauty, gained thanks to plenty of "racaktox," a variation of the most powerful botulinum toxin type A, had crumbled through an excess of make-up. Her appearance showed the consecutive late nights partying with drugs and drinking. She was exhausted and a wreck in appearance and health. Crying, she screamed at the other fairy:

"That's enough! Do you want to humiliate me even more? Evil, cruel, heartless woman!"

The winner felt sorry for the loser. As neither could ever die or change position, that had been just one more of the innumerable battles in the grand roll of fame.

The Fairy Queen of Easy Fame moved away, swearing to return, while the Fairy Queen of Real Fame went to encourage those who deservedly obtained success in life.

CHAPTER XII

THE CASTLE WALL, THE MARCH OF THE WORMS AND THE GUARDIANS

The day after the clash between the Fairy Queens of Fame, in the centre of the Green Valley, none of the events seemed to provoke any kind of life or activity in the Castle of Western Music. There was no soldier or guard visible on the battlements

Around five o'clock in the morning on an infamous night, the four hundred worms were getting closer and closer. The Oppressive Forces of Music's high command knew that the seven sides of the Castle were absolutely equal in form, power and defence. So, they opted for concentrating their forces on just one side. Only one part of the right flank and another on the left began a trajectory to surround and besiege the great heptagon. Soon it would be embraced by two tentacles of a huge dark stain that wished to devour it.

The march of the worms was dirty for several reasons. First of all, as already said, because they exhaled a slimy acid that put an end to life of the flora and fauna below their huge bodies. Secondly, because they defecated almost all the time. They never stopped eating and there's no digestive system that can utilize one hundred per cent of what it ingests. With the exception of the milk from the arum lily that Violet drank, there is no food that is totally utilizable. And thus, the totally deformed remains of notes, women and baboons processed in the oesophagi, stomachs and intestines, which weren't even good for manure through being so toxic, were dumped on the trails of death and dirt.

Coming after the worms, the rest of the army was marching rhythmically. Clouds of *coorraína* were sprayed with more frequency as they approached the battlements.

At six o'clock precisely, another dark, reddish stain polluted the sky that had barely become light. A large squadron of air force was arriving, similar to the one that attacked the flower ball, though in far greater numbers. They were well armed with weapons and ideas of perversity. The riders, or pilots, were baboons which were screaming and swearing at anyone and everyone. Their strategic objective was to do the first bombardment of the Castle and begin to undermine its defences from within. They approached and, when no one was looking, spat at the lowly infantry marching beside the worms. They would soon be entering the Castle's airspace, passing over the battlements.

Two hundred metres, one hundred metres, two metres and they were flying over the castle walls. They must have been going at a speed of three hundred kilometres an hour. They pointed their weapons, laughing and swearing at the world around them.

That was when twenty four black faces appeared from one the parapets of the seven exterior towers, the seven interior towers and the ten smaller towers. No one on the ground would have been able to see them because the towers were very high. They were about six metres tall with impeccable hearing, holding huge hammers made of some unknown metal that must have weighed two hundred kilos. They had strong arms, eagle eyes and such sharp ears that they didn't need to see to know what was happening there. Even so, their expressions were severe. They were the twenty four guardians of the towers. They were the wisest and most respected instrument tuners in the worlds. Many millennia before they had been graced with the title of Master Guardians of Instruments and the Towers. They were old, noble men of undetermined age who devoted their lives to watching over and inspiring the master instrument makers in the Kingdoms. They also worked to improve the sense of hearing of beings and make orchestras more finely tuned.

Their arms moved and hammered the twenty four tuning forks the size of a building, which floated between the Towers. In other words, they activated the giant gold tuning forks that each tower housed. The extremities of their prongs were twenty metres below the top of each tower. Each tuning fork was suspended in the air because the end opposite the two prongs passed through a disc of dense light four-metres thick, with a diameter of fifty metres. What can magic of the science of obtaining light with controlled density not do? These discs of light were an old gift from the ancient music spirits, and from evolutionary planes that our imagination cannot yet reach.

They were the scientists of the advanced occult. They were the admirable Alchemists of Photons. Made in solar forges, the tuning forks vibrated in the frequencies of each note of the Tower.

It was the first time in the history of the Kingdom that the tuning forks had resonated. Each one of them vibrated at the fundamental frequency of its own note and also in an infinite polyphonic composition and superposition of harmonies. This generated a frequency field that began on the parapets of the battlements and formed a dome that covered the entire Castle of Western Music.

It wasn't a field of energy or magic, because even the most powerful field of energy or magic can be drained or surpassed by a greater energy or superior magic. However, in the plane of the kingdom of Music, a frequency field like that is indestructible because nothing from light or darkness vibrates like it. Thus, everything not of the same syntony would find in it a decomposing end. Would find molecular chaos and vital chaos.

That is what happened to the winged dragons, which in milliseconds had stopped vibrating, and therefore existing. Where did their spirits go? It is not for this story to reveal this.

The same happened with the catapults, which had come to try to throw bubbles of pitch over the castle walls. As for the baboons and other partners, when they noticed the extermination of part of the air force and the waste of the malevolent ammunition, they began to throw tantrums. If it hadn't been so noisy, it would at least have been funny or ridiculous. There were notes, women, baboons and pianolas howling, jumping, screaming, floundering in an attack of collective infantile whining. When not terrorizing or when losing, evil is always pathetic.

But, even when evil yields, withdraws, cries or chickens out, it does not give up. When the impact of the loss and the collective frenzy had passed, the infantry captains gave the order for some baboons that had the advantage of strength and size, being more like gorillas than baboons, to stab their chainsaws into the behinds of the Worms.

The acid from their slimy emissions corroded and rendered the jagged-edged, sharp blades of the electric saws useless at once. Some were pulverized into vapour; others into caustic acid which blinded the baboons when it sprayed into their eyes.

The Worms howled in pain and raised their fronts from the ground like snakes ready to strike. When they fell back down, the whole Valley shook. Enraged, they flicked out their tongues and made new victims of their own army, who tried to fight back in vain. They were devoured in an instant. The worms then recommenced their funereal march as if they were war tanks the size of crawling whales, if these existed.

With its rave beat and clouds of *coorraína,* the music recommenced. The infantry had resumed their bellowing of "courage" and shouting in four-four time.:

- Harh! Harh! Harh! Harh!!!   Harh! Harh! Harh! Harh!!! Harh! Harh! Harh! Hah!!!

The guardians of the Towers stood ready to hammer the tuning forks once more.

The Worms were already close to the colossal castle walls. Thirty of them disobeyed the instructions of their captains. One of them decided to test the resistance of the wall; another, between intrepidness and hesitation, got ready to climb it. This was fatal. The sticky tongue in contact with the unique material of the walls caused a chemical reaction typical of batteries. Ten million volts, though. The walls were the positive and the tongue the negative. In contact with the soil of the Valley, a current of more than one hundred thousand amps encircled the huge body. It tried to recoil its tongue, but the tongue was melting and fusing with the walls. Other wretched invertebrates were literally fried from the inside out. The very high intensity of the flow of electrons toasted their internal organs. Parts of their bodies exploded and in the end there were just burnt stains on the walls and dead grass.

Some worms with their tongues recoiled began to climb in the way that caterpillars climb trees. They advanced thirty metres when the same electro-chemical reactions began. However, they were disconnected from the ground and believed that the deadly current would not flow or pass through their bodies. They were wrong. The electric energy power was close to one million volts, because the area of contact of their acid, slimy bodies was greater than the area of contact of their tongues. This high voltage broke the dielectric of the air. In other words, the same electrostatic phenomenon happened that occurs in the clouds when the difference in   electric power is very great and the atmosphere is ionized. The resistance of the air diminishes and the electric current circulates in the form of lightning. But in this case several bolts sprang from their bodies. Some went straight into the ground. Others hit the baboons, men, women of the Oppressive Forces army. The climbing worms and the others that were hit were also burnt alive.

"Numbskulls! Imbeciles! Idiots! The order was to burrow. Burrow now! Or I'll be burrowing holes in you," yelled our old and unbeloved pianola.

Its vapours and black smoke increased. It began its own funereal music, which left no doubt at all regarding the remaining three hundred and sixty worms. They began to burrow into the soil together, two hundred metres from each other. They worked efficiently and quickly. They advanced frenetically and burrowed into the soil. They were soon eating earth and anything alive that lived in the soil. They defecated what they ingested almost instantaneously.

If the plan were to work, they would dig three hundred and sixty access tunnels under the walls for the Oppressive Forces. At first everything went well for them. As they began their excavations at an attack angle of forty-five degrees, almost two hundred and eighty three metres later they were passing at a depth of two hundred metres from the line of the walls. However, they were much deeper down than they realised and twenty of them that didn't notice in time were toasted by the effects of electricity.

The rest turned back, but digging horizontally. When they were three hundred metres from the subterranean walls, they changed the angle of attack of the excavations to eighty degrees more. And they accelerated. They went down now devouring the earth at a rate of two point seven metres per second. In other words, they dug ten kilometres an hour. When they reached a new depth for going under the walls, they encountered the subterranean walls again. This time they were smarter and more decisive. They didn't touch the walls and went back again, to go down perpendicularly. Now they were digging into solid, hard rock. Their speed fell off. Even so, they were faster diggers than any ever reported in any newspaper on Earth or in any fairy story.

Sixteen long hours later, they were a hundred kilometres deep, and still they hadn't reached the beginning of the walls.

In fact, the walls began metres below the semi-viscous limit of the tectonic plate with the sea of interior magma of the planet. The temperature was close to six thousand degrees Celsius, but since the material the walls were made of had been formed in solar forges, that temperature was refreshing for them.

The same could not be said of the giant worms. They didn't have sweat glands and were so intoxicated by rotten food that they couldn't feel heat or cold. When they realized they were digging their own graves, it was already too late. They melted in the sea of magma of the Kingdom of the Seven Moons. And thus it was that their species died out for good.

On the surface, it was midnight when the generals, captains, lieutenants, sergeants, privates and weapons bearers of the Oppressive Forces, who were impatiently waiting for news of the worms, saw hot, red lava being expelled from the holes that had been dug.

Those close by were toasted by the mini volcanoes and rivers of lava that were running along the trails of death left by the worms. When these reached the limits of the desert the lava was already almost cold and solidifying. And the holes were completely sealed off.

This was the response of renovation that the Heart of the Seven Kingdoms was giving. This was because, over time, the trails of lava would become fertile soil. Once more there was a frenzy of whining and anger from the invading army. When they stopped that ridiculous horror show, their hate and spite knew no limits.

"Wretches! Damn Castle! Get everyone! Torture them all! Enslave them all! I want minds, bodies and souls! I want plenty of souls! All the music! All the notes! All the instruments! I want the guardians! I want them! I want them! I'm going to spit and dine in the gardens of this pigsty!" screamed the pianola.

The screams were taken up by the others. Seconds later a great chorus began. It was the chorus of the enslaved notes, full of pain and revolt. The instruments and catapults were already in position and they all began the attack against the same area of the castle wall.

Notes and more notes of sadness and hate were thrown and collided at more than a thousand kilometres an hour against the wall, which seemed to feel nothing. Six hours later, the first rays of sun found a battlefield where only one side was attacking without mercy and with no letup. The day proceeded, the dirt spread like an oil spill from a platform on a beautiful coral reef. The green of that region of the Valley disappeared, succumbing to the pollution that despair and ignorance bring. The bombardment didn't ease off even for a second, but the walls resisted. For how long? The answer was connected to how long the Oppressive Forces would take by the method of trial and error to find the right frequency of pain, sadness and hate that would wound the fibres of sensibility of the thick walls.

Many winged dragons were flying over the castle to ensure that no one would dare to run away or get help. That aerial patrol was unnecessary because the Castle was already well surrounded and none of the occupants would leave.

Six hours went by and nothing unusual happened. Another six hours passed and the day darkened at the saddest sunset in the history of the Kingdom of the Seven Moons. Darkness fell. The Seven Moons were in pre-mourning and didn't want to shine so as not to help the artillery's aim. Even in the total darkness, the Oppressive Forces refused to stop. They would die and use up all their resources if necessary, but they would not move from the spot without absolute annihilation. God help the poor women, men, baboons or notes that showed signs of tiredness and didn't make up for it with *corraina* and the strong alcohol served in trucks that look like our water tankers. If they didn't do this they were whipped at once. And if they thought for even one second about deserting, they would become immediate ammunition or fuel for the pianolas.

At the beginning of the second day, a horrific crack was heard. It pained some and was celebrated by many. A part of the wall more or less ten metres high and equidistant from the two towers was seriously breached. After several attempts, the Oppressive Forces were arriving close to their objective.

They celebrated with a collective roar even louder than when they were yelling or whining. The attack stopped for two minutes. A crack five metres long and two metres wide could be seen forming vertically. The wall seemed to be alive and expressing a feeling of pain from the deep one-metre cut in its structure. A new order was heard. The artillery then focussed on the crack.

Two Guardians of two of the Towers adjusted the angle of the tuning forks as much as they could. They made a huge effort and this represented less than half a degree in inclination. Once again they began to hammer the tuning forks. This meant that on that side of the Castle the frequency field began lower than the line of the parapet. But the crack was very close to ground level and the frequency field was very rarefied in that region. If the Guardians had inclined the tuning forks even more, the air space would have been unprotected and they would no longer be sustained by magic when vibrating at maximum amplitude.

So, this is what could be done at that moment. The new artillery charge arrived along with the weakened frequency field. A new impasse of force formed. However, it was clear that in this intensity other cracks could appear. And it was not known how long the injured wall that was being supported could resist.

Hope now lay in a possible and victorious counter attack from the Castle Forces. However, this didn't happen, and there was not the least indication that it would.

CHAPTER XIII

THE MISSION

Two and a half days before the partial splitting of the wall had been the decisive moment when Violet had escaped from the Fairy Queen of Easy Fame and her slave rats. It was a night when the trio walked to the point of exhaustion. As they had found no shelter, they slept a few hours in the lower branches of an oak tree. For Violet and Joaquina the night had been very uncomfortable. But Pedrão didn't mind. As a butterfly, he found trees great spots for rest.

Aside from the fact that on the two following nights Joaquina managed to take them to comfortable caves, with a floor of soft sand, the two days passed without any novelty, besides hunger, that deserved mention or comment.

It's true, Violet's hunger was already a problem, but as far as thirst was concerned, there was nothing to worry about. Throughout the entire walk they came upon brooks or passed by springs and bubbling waters. And so, each time she sipped the spurting drops or dipped her face into the brooks, Violet learned that we can tolerate hunger, but that thirst is unbearable. This brought such thoughts to her mind as:

"Thank you little spring. Water is wealth. Why are the rivers where I live dirty?"

Joaquina, Violet and Pedrão continued to the limits of their energy and the forest became increasingly similar to a vast flooded region, the Pantanal in Mato Grosso, Brazil.

This time they walked in silence. They didn't argue, provoke or try to be funny.

Flooded and dark. This was what the Nameless Marsh was like. Many spiders' webs and carnivorous plants lay in wait for careless butterflies. Anacondas eager to devour even a weaned calf could be found amidst the damp, submersed vegetation. Alligators with bad breath, poisonous vipers and wily ocelots were always after their meal of the day. But what alligators, vipers, ocelots and constrictors really feared was the great jaguar, four meters tall, with four hundred kilos of muscles – besides another two hundred of bones, fat and skin.

Incidentally, they say that its coat was softer and shinier than any velvet or satin. However, its breath, temperament, claws, and teeth were more hostile than the giant porcupines that also lived there, or even more dangerous than the barbed wire used in restricted military zones. Nothing living in that swamp was a match for it. And the jaguar, unless its mouth was watering for food, avoided all contact. It remained undisturbed in some creek or dark lake. It really wouldn't be prudent to disturb it.

The Nameless Marsh was next to the Marsh of the New World Legends, visited by *sacis*[5], bogeymen, will o' the wisp and other sources of inspiration for indigenous beliefs in South America, as well as other sources of Inca, Maya, Aztec legends besides those of the North-American Indians,

---

[5] One-legged mythical men from Brazilian folklore, who can appear and disappear at will

the Cherokees and Sioux, occasionally flying, running by and whispering their matters, entertainments, drum rhythms and music.

But these sources of legends and myths did not interfere with the Nameless Marsh. They just came to savour the silence. The silence that would be assassinated if the Oppressive Forces of Music were successful in the conquest of the Castle. They planned to raze it to the ground and build a giant complex of phonographic factories of all media, surrounded by music and party venues never before seen in the entire universe. They would also be installing a great plantation of the vegetable that produced the active ingredient of *coorraína*. They knew that the water of that Marsh was the best possible. So, why not control it? After all, whoever controls water has power. It would be from there that they would supply and control the music of all kingdoms. Even the powerful jaguar could do nothing to prevent it if its peace and quiet and the kingdom were annihilated. Nor would it be able to do anything against the infestation of rats and cockroaches that, eager for waste of every type, would infest the ex-Nameless Marsh.

In this marsh, something greater guided the steps of Violet, Joaquina and Pedrão so that they would not be accidentally or intentionally attacked. And so it was that by the end of the day Violet had arrived at her inevitable encounter with destiny.

At the edge of the Nameless Marsh there was a big lake called Aquancarau, which in the language of the ancient beings of the Kingdom meant End of the Beginning of the Waters of Life. It was an unusual lake, very similar to the Okavango Delta, in Namibia, on the African continent of the Kingdom of the Blue Earth. Just as in the Okavango Delta, in Africa, all the rivers and creeks in a great area flowed into it.

It had deep, mysterious sections. But for the most part, it was shallow and was sixty kilometres at its widest. Lake Aquancarau lived in an eternal cycle of fullness in the rainy summers and shrinkage in the dry winters. Part of the thawing snows from the hills that marked the limits of the Green Valley fed around thirty per cent of the lake with their clean waters.

The rest came from two hydrographic basins whose lost rivers never found their way to the sea and ended their lives as rivers of running water in the lake. Thus, an entire ecosystem, depended the water cycle.

Lake Aquancarau marked the frontier of the Nameless Marsh with two further marshes, as well as the Marsh of the Legends of the New World. At its southern extremity, where it was at its narrowest, a desert began that extended for more than five hundred kilometres until the green of the flora and the colours of the flowers returned, establishing the seasons. This was the Desert of Dead Music, where nothing vibrated.

But neither the surrounding Marsh nor the Desert and even less Lake Aquancarau were more important than the balance of the cycles of waters and the cycle of music of the marshes, which reigned up to then. If this was broken, the consequences would be catastrophic for at least half the continent.

When the trio crossed the final barrier of forest, one hundred and eighty metres from one of the shores of the lake, Violet let out a scream that, to everyone's luck, was promptly stifled by Joaquina, as quick as a hemidemisemiquaver.

"No!!!!!!!!!!!!!!!!!!!!!! You'll get us killed!!!!!!!!!!!!!!!!!!!!"

Pedrão and Joaquina pushed Violet to the flooded ground just at the moment they would have been discovered.

On the diffuse threshold between the Lake and the flooded lands of the Nameless Marsh, the most majestic fairy or queen was in a dreadful, fearful and aberrant situation.

Standing up, she was singing to preserve her own life and the life of the Kingdom of the Seven Moons. In no other situation could anyone appreciate a melody of such strength and health. Her voice was supplanting even the voice of the Fairy Queen of the Marsh of Love.

The image that Violet had seen some time before, brought by the flower eagle, when she received food from the arum lily, was nothing like the vision of the Goddess, Muse, Fairy Queen of the Music of Seven Notes, or simply queen, as they called her. However, she was imprisoned by the inconceivable and the outrageous.

A dome or a semi-bubble of pitch the size of a cathedral enveloped her, waiting to collapse on top of her. Approximately two hundred reptiles similar to adult komodo dragons, though twice the size, encircled the bubble, ridden by baboons. These dragons and baboons were the elite secret police of the Oppressive Forces of Music.

Like their distant cousins in Indonesia, in the Kingdom of the Blue Earth, their mouths held a fatal type of bacteria and poison that infected anyone even slightly bitten. Death was inevitable because, unless the Queen of Music herself administered the remedy, there was no known cure. The dragons of the Kingdom of the Seven Moons had been trained in the School of Perverse Singing, in the Morbid Singing module. Their long, forked, snake-like tongues moved, intoning the funeral song, "The Laughter of the Lizards".

In the meantime, the baboons sprayed, spat and vomited every kind of music of the lowest category. They went from hard pornography, to the worst sweaty, booming funk. Many pianolas helped in this circle and didn't stop for a minute. They expelled and executed music of despair, apathy and rage in all styles, even that usually called classical music. However, the pianolas knew that far more important than the style of music was the reason for its existence. Thus, in the attempt to confuse, many of them hid their worst intentions in the form of refined concerts.

This infernal musical cauldron re-fed itself in a continuous effort to crush the Fairy Queen inside the bubble. Hundreds of winged dragons ridden by baboons made the aerial attack. But the biggest pressure of all came from the being above the bubble. This being, which could not be defined as a fairy, but which demanded to be so called, proclaimed herself the Fairy Queen of Totalitarian Music.

She knew how to seduce, and could take on for a certain time the most beautiful form she desired. Months later, however, the mask would fall and she would return to what she really was and liked being.

In this phase, her face was beautiful at night, but during the day she would compete with the Medusa of Greek myths for horror and ugliness. From waist to head she measured some four and a half metres. Her trunk and internal organs were those of a woman. However, instead of legs, she had twelve brown tentacles, eighteen metres long, full of vents like red cornets, which could both blow out and suck in. For the health of her spirit and body she had inside her the worst of all music.

Some say that she had been one of the most talented and beautiful fairies and one of the Fairy Queen's main allies. However, at some moment long ago in time, she had allowed herself to be seduced by dark forces. Vanity led to pride, and pride to selfishness. As this feeds unmeasured ambition and this is the mother of tyranny, she had throughout the centuries become a heinous being with a thousand faces and forms that she had chosen to be. Like all beings, she was the fruit of herself.

With a hand of rancour and iron and an army feared for its brutality, she commanded the Oppressive Forces of Music, openly admitting her hate and disrespect for all that is good, for health, liberty and responsibility. For her, the most toxic and indigestible fluid – and which also gave her stomach ache – was that of love.

Faced with this perverse pressure, the unescorted good Queen tried to resist. Her song created a light and a field of music that impeded her capture. She was a prisoner, but not defeated. She couldn't free herself but her enemies didn't crush her. She showed signs of wear and tiredness noticed only by Violet's scared little heart.

Their hearts were connected. And the girl already had a notion of what she should do. It's just that she didn't know how.

For half an hour of agony nothing unusual occurred, until the Fairy Queen of Totalitarian Music, floating thanks to the bad smelling gases expelled through her vents, abandoned the top of the pitch dome of despair and proclaimed:

"I didn't have to have a son that I brought up and fed for him to be fat, dull and lazy. Let's go, Magmamute! I have more things to do!"

"Aw, mummy. I'm sorry, but not so much."

Coming out of the lake and jumping over the bubble, a wet thing appeared composed of neck, a man's head and body of an octopus with twelve tentacles. It was a giant with a swollen head, supported by a fat, wrinkled neck that sprouted from an octopus body.

He must have been eighty metres from head to the tip of the tentacles and weighed one hundred and forty tons. Like the Giant Worms, his hunger was excessive. To prevent him from bursting, his mother still breast-fed him. Only this way did he remain for days without devouring the vital energy of any creature unfortunate enough to be grabbed by his tentacles of out-of-tune sounds. His insatiable hunger was for power and control – and this the sour milk from his mother's breast could supply.

"That's right, son. Squeeze it out!"

The Fairy Queen felt the heavy weight and everyone could notice.

"That's it, son. That's right! Squeeze it more."

The creature made a phenomenal effort and sprayed music of the darkness through the cornets in his suckers, encouraging those who were participating in the cruel attack. The Totalitarian Fairy Queen also squeezed the side of the bubble.

It was left to the Fairy Queen of Music to sing with more strength. But by now her fatigue was clear to see. Even so, she did not give up. When the bubble stretched all around her, she made up for it with more energy.

"You damned wretch! You have to give up! It's hopeless. The Kingdom of the Blue Earth is almost entirely mine! I want this and all the others! Everything is mine! Do you understand? There's no hope for you! Give up, and I'll spare your ridiculous musical life. Give up!"

The Fairy Queen lost neither her serenity nor her elegance. But her strength had run out.

"Where are the tarantulas? Where are they?" said the furious Fairy Queen of Totalitarian Music.

An army of a thousand tarantulas the size of tortoises appeared to spit out melodies that formed webs of despair. At the same moment, another division of baboons, men and women carrying trumpets as if they were bayonets positioned themselves to execute their diabolical sounds.

As in the attack on the Castle – where at that moment the fight was intensified, increasing the crack in the wall – the strategy was to bombard on the physical, psychological and spiritual planes. It was beginning to work.

The Fairy Queen of Music sighed a deep, sad lament. That was enough for her knees to buckle and she had to support herself with her hands on the ground so that her face wouldn't smack against the mixture of mud and pitch that was seeping through the walls of the bubble at the points where the musical field was weakest.

She resumed her singing, but the bubble was already close to crushing her. A great collective roar was heard, like that provoked by the ball almost going in at the end of a championship. Her enemies were already celebrating and savouring the taste of her fall. Magmamute was hoping that his mother would give her to him to chew to the last splinter of her Fairy bones.

"Forget about weakening her, squash this bitch! Trumpets, let's go! Use your heads, notes.

Far from there, in the Green Valley, the crack was frightening. Soon there would be a hole big enough to invade the Castle.

In the centre of combat, in the Nameless Marsh, the Fairy Queen of Music made a futile

effort to get up. The weight of hopelessness, which is the heaviest weight of all weights, bowed the Fairy Queen's back and shoulders. The attackers were laughing the laugh of the evil who are thirsty for the pain of the torture of others. This would be the great banquet at the feast of darkness.

A tear shining with violet light ran down the good fairy's face and touched the muddy

ground. A small, fragile violet bloomed there at once.

"It's not right. It's not right. Give me that, I'll help. I'll take it to her!"

Joaquina had no time to do anything. Violet pulled the small, final magic tuning fork from Joaquina's leg and took off. She was running so fast that not even her father or any boy from school would be able to catch her.

"But what are you doing? Have you lost your senses, girl??????????????????"

"She really is clueless!" said Pedrão in surprise. "So, are we just going to stay here watching?"

"No way!!!!!!!!!!!!!!!!!!!!!! Now I'm really angry!!!!!!!!!!!!!!!!!"

They shot after the girl, who had the element of surprise in her favour. In less than four seconds, Violet was running between pianolas, men, women and baboons. One of pianolas did shout to alert their allies but the noise level was so high that two more precious seconds passed before the first enemies noticed a small, agile and determined girl dressed as a princess running in that grim battle field. When she got near the spiders, a dozen of them formed a barrier. But Violet was very good at tig and was always the best at not being caught. She threatened to turn right, feigned going to the left and broke through the circle spinning, without even being touched by any spider claw or hair.

"What's going on? They told me she was dead. Whoever lied to me will pay! Damned Fairy Queen of Easy Fame! She didn't get her and pretended she had. She'll pay! Get her," thundered the Fairy Queen of Totalitarian music, when she understood the weakness and lies of her cousin, the Fairy Queen of Easy Fame.

Violet accelerated and propelled herself over a dragon's back and jumped three metres out of reach of its forked tongue. She was almost there. There were just twenty metres left, when she was surrounded by a legion of hemidemisemi quavers with glassy eyes, and no pupils, and by ten emperor wasps. She came to a halt to study her next move. There wasn't much time. Three dragons were coming behind her, eager for the girl's human flesh. They were salivating, while the baboons riding them shouted:

"She's mine! She's mine!"

The biggest dragon blew into the eyes of his rival on the left, temporarily blinding it. It scraped his tongue across the eyes of his competitor on the right and threw its body of hard, scaly skin against the enemy. The rival dragon fell, rolling to the side and its weight crushed the baboon rider.

"What's this, you stupid animals? Stop and hunt down that girl once and for all!" roared the Fairy Queen of Oppressive Music.

The good Fairy Queen, her face pale and running with sweat, realized, worried about Violet, that this was a critical moment. But she could do nothing, other than sing in the girl's direction, opening up a space in the pitch bubble. Violet's instincts were telling her to go back. She wouldn't be able to get through the hemidemisemi quavers and the ten-centimetre wasps. That was when Joaquina threw herself headfirst, colliding with the musical note barrier and Pedrão sprayed the pollen of a rare flower into the eyes of five wasps. It was a secret weapon he carried on his feet, a powerful sleep-inducing substance. The butterfly became entangled in combat with the remaining wasps.

Taking advantage of the confusion, Violet jumped over the barrier of confused notes. She advanced towards the break in the bubble. Joaquina started fighting the notes. They didn't have the same resistance, but were much quicker than she was. As they were greater in number, her end, as well as that of Pedrão, was near. But this didn't matter to her or to Pedrão. They wanted to buy more precious, necessary time for Violet. The biggest of the three dragons knocked over Pedrão, Joaquina, wasps and musical notes. Ten metres, nine, eight, five and a half, three, two. There were just two metres left for the fastest eight-year-old girl in the Kingdom of the Blue Earth, and she threw herself head first.

"Ahhhhhhhhhhhhhhhhhhhhhhhhhhhh!

That was what she screamed when the dragon's hot forked tongue encircled her left ankle. It began to recoil its saliva-covered tongue – full of lethal poison – and drag her towards its jaws. The girl was powerless and her tiny pianist's hands couldn't grab hold of anything to prevent the massacre.

"You can devour her. She's your reward," roared the hoarse, out-of-tune voice of the Fairy Queen of Oppressive Music, who was also flying towards Violet and getting closer. Just one metre now separated Violet from the smile of the reptile that would tear her to pieces and eat her in just one mouthful.

"Spare her∞ ♪ ♫ ♥ ! I surrender∞ ♪ ♫ ♥ ! I give up everything∞ ♪ ♫ ♥ ! I surrender∞ ♪ ♫ ♥ ! It's over∞ ♪ ♫ ♥ ! I've lost∞ ♪ ♫ ♥ !

It was the voice of the Fairy Queen who, through the power of her authority, made time stand still at that moment. However, after two interminable seconds, an unquestionable counter-order was heard:

"Ahhhhhhhhhhhhhhhh! Forget about sparing her. Pullets are pullets. I want it all. I want all the souls, notes and desires. Keep going. Ahhhhhhhhhhhhhhh!"

When the Dantesque, infernal attack recommenced, Violet could hear the Fairy Queen:

"Magic gift∞ ♪ ♫ ♥ ! Magic gift∞ ♪ ♫ ♥ !

She understood at once. She pulled a magic slipper from her right foot and threw it straight down the dragon's throat. Its tongue released Violet's ankle because at the same time the slipper vibrated like a xylophone in a frequency of love. This was the worst of the worst chilli peppers for dragons. Choking, it rolled and twisted on the ground. Its baboon struggled, but ended up squashed.

With her ankle bleeding from the bitter acid of the dragon's tongue, Violet leapt up to the bubble, which then closed. She embraced the Fairy and said not in the voice of a heroine but of one who needs protection:

"I've brought this to help. It's magic."

The girl threw the little tuning fork to the ground. It vibrated magically and made time itself slow down. At this rhythm, seconds last for years and Violet was able to have all the time in the world to think, feel, decide and be thankful for her short life of eight years.

Outside the bubble, Joaquina was being defeated on the ground. It took three hemidemisemiquavers to keep her stretched out while a fourth was strangling her. Pedrão had defeated two enemies, but the wasps had torn his lovely, fragile wings to shreds. He couldn't fly any longer and lay exhausted, waiting for the wasp sting that would puncture his butterfly neck. The end for both was announced in the next two seconds. Far from there, the castle walls had been breached and a four-metre hole had formed in them.

"My dear. Very, very good. You have excelled yourself. Now, wish for your own salvation. Go home. I'm commanding you∞ ♪ ♫ ♥ !," said the Fairy Queen to Violet, inside the bubble. The child's eyes were wet and another blue-ish tear watered a newborn violet. Soon afterwards, her eyes went dark. The poisonous bacteria of the dragon's saliva were already having an effect. Violet felt a pain in her bones that gradually found the way to her soul, which also ached terribly.

She looked at Pedrão, at the Fairy and at her good companion Joaquina. The memory of her mother's face and love were lights in her torment. The strength of her father's music, the energy of her grandparents and everything good she'd had in her life gave her a unique serenity. She was riddled with pain, but she didn't care.

"Let the Kingdom of Music...let the Little Planet be saved".

This was her last wish before the darkness closed her eyes and life left her.

CHAPTER XIV

SOME REASONS

So small and with so much energy, the tuning fork rang out in G major, granting Violet's great wish. Initially, an infra-red light, in other words, electromagnetic radiation the length of a wave beyond the capabilities of human vision, flooded the bubble from inside out. Seconds later, the light became red. Then, pink. The same pink as the most charming roses. The immense light ran through the rest of the colours of the rainbow. It shone for a long time in the colour violet, alternating with an irradiation of sky blue. Then the sound of G major increased and the light became rosy pink again.

With a mother's tenderness, the Fairy Queen embraced the girl who lay unconscious. The Fairy of Oppressive Music's eyes almost popped out of her head. She was the true vision of Medusa. She wanted to scream the command to retreat. She only wished it, because there was no time for anything else.

Sounds of crystal breaking, silver cutlery clanking in the kitchen, volcanoes erupting, and tremors of tsunamis shook the foundations of the Kingdom. The sound went back to G major and the light passed through yellow, orange and then rosy pink. But this time it looked like a gigantic soap bubble that was growing in size and luminous intensity. One could almost see the traces of photons and their luminous heads moving at the speed of light.

It was like an explosion of a mini supernova. Magmamute's tentacles were toasted and then he had the same end. The Tyrant Fairy cried out on seeing her son's agony, but did nothing. She flew far away, removing herself from the scene. After all, she didn't like him very much. He was nothing more than an instrument at her service.

The bubble of rosy light became a ball of light and swept over the entire Marsh. Along with the other elements of the evil army, the bubble of pitch disintegrated. Saving Pedrão and Joaquina, the magic light reconstituted the valiant butterfly's wings and Joaquina's broken leg. Reaching more than a kilometre in diameter, it became a bubble once more and expanded in every direction, even reaching the vicinity of the Castle of Occidental Music, to then envelop it. A new roar was heard throughout the continent: it was the people of the Castle who had come out of their state of apathy.

The rosy light had another surprising effect: it activated the intelligent and regenerating polymers that made up the material of the Castle wall. It healed over. The photons of luminous explosion woke up the polymers, which for their part massaged the powerful metal alloy, and energised its mineral life. The hole of more than forty metres began to close and crush any intruder who dared to go through it. In a minute, there was nothing to show that at a point equidistant from the two Towers, there had once been a passage for the invading troops.

It was the first time in millennia that the guardians of the towers had smiled. Not that they were unhappy, but it was their way to be too serious and focused to smile.

"Ahhhhhhhhhhhhhhhhhh!!!!!!!!!!!!!"

A new collective roar was heard, and this time it was like a goal that turned the game around that echoed through the Green Valley.

"Wake up!!!!!!!!!!!!!!!!!!!!!!!!!!!! To the castle!!!!!!!!!!!!!!!!!!!!!!!!!!!! Defend the walls!!!!!!!!!!!!!!!!!!!!"

In the centre of the Marsh the fantastic tuning fork consumed the last molecule, then the last atom and even the last subatomic particle of itself. It had fully accomplished its noble mission. And in its last breath of vibration, in its swan song, a human face formed between its prongs. Looking at the Fairy Queen of Music and blessing everyone, it disappeared or disintegrated, perhaps to live on other planes without pain or despair.

The Nameless Marsh was like an abandoned field of war. But the magic of the tuning fork had cleaned much of the visible dirt. However, the pain would remain, roaming like dense mist for some time. A much greater pain was felt by the Fairy Queen of Music, Joaquina and Pedrão.

Not so long ago, they used to say to boys in the Kingdom of the Blue Earth:

"Hey, are you crying? Real men don't cry"

Happily, the culture of the beings on planet earth has already evolved enough to know that men, like women, can cry. Physical pain is terrible, but nothing compares with the pain of remorse of the soul. For this, no painkiller, tranquiliser, anti-inflammatory or even morphine can offer a resolution.

Pedrão the butterfly was crying. Butterflies, like everything alive or one day intends to live, also cry. And Pedrão was crying from remorse at not having been stronger and saved his friend Violet. Joaquina was crying in despair. And the Fairy was looking at everyone, with the deepest Fairy sadness. The universe itself seem to lose colour and becomes washed out when a Fairy like the Fairy Queen of Music reaches this level of sadness. A level that could drown even the sea.

In the Fairy's arms, the girl's body was going cold and her cheeks, formerly so rosy, were as white as a sheet.

Up to that moment, she had tried all the magic she knew. She had sung music of health and life, which had no effect due to the advanced stage of the poison produced by the dragon bacteria.

As there was nothing more she knew how to or could do, the most angelic and powerful Fairy Queen in the Kingdom of Occidental Music lay the girl on the ground, knelt and prayed. Yes, she prayed as we all pray when we're in danger, despair or depression. She prayed with her pure soul, wise mind and life of feats and heroic missions. Would she be heard? Would she be listened to? Would her prayer be answered?

Very far from there, in a flat in the centre of a city where millions of people lived in thousands of flats, a woman was having terrible nightmares. She was writhing in bed in her sleep. Her womb was aching but even so she didn't wake up. Sleep and dreams were maximum security prisons for the spirit of Violet's mother. She would never remember her dreams from that night. Nor the nightmare, the worst that a mother or father could have. She dreamt that she was losing her daughter Violet. In this tragic dream, she also prayed, asking God to take care of her daughter. A tear ran down the face of the sleeping woman. It was a tear that contained a small violet luminescence. Even though she was sleeping, the woman sighed and dreamt from then on a dream of peace.

Violet's mother's tear crossed the dimensions at such speed that the Fairy Queen herself could not explain it. The mother's tear ran at the speed of a mother's desire to save her daughter. It leapt over dimensional obstacles and in an instant was floating in front of the Fairy Queen.

She started singing again, and her voice hit timbres that no soprano could reach. She sang Celtic songs and many others celebrating life, and finally sang the lullabies of mothers from all cultures when calming their babies.

The tear grew and fell like a summer shower over the girl's body, while a strong brightness enveloped her. The laughter of three-year-olds and babies could be heard in all corners of the Marsh. Church bells, train whistles and summer ice-cream van horns invaded the air.

"Ring a ring of roses..."

This and may other children's rhymes made their presence known until Violet opened her sweet eyes. Her soul or spirit had returned and the terrible cocktail of bacteria had been expelled. Her damaged and dead cells were miraculously revived. The girl just said: "Are there any beans? I'm hungry."

CHAPTER XV

OTHER REASONS

There had never been a fairy, a musical note and a butterfly so happy all at the same time. Just as there had never been a girl so famished.

"My dear, this is not your country∞ ♪ ♫ ♥ ! But if everything works out you'll soon be eating beans ∞ ♪ ♫ ♥ !"

"What are beans?" asked Pedrão.

"Stay quiet!!!!!!!!!!!!!!!!!! Can't you see that I want to hug her??????????????"said Joaquina, overcome with emotion.

Violet got to her feet and received the tightest hug in the world. Pedrão didn't respect Joaquina's desire to hug Violet and hovered around waiting for a chance to give the girl a kiss. At that moment, Violet felt just one pain, the lack of home-cooked food: black beans, well seasoned, and with plenty of broth, served with rice, kale, and french fries would be better than any magic milk from an arum lily.

But Violet would have to quell that desire. So she had no option but to feed herself from a honeycomb. While she hungrily sucked the energy from the flowers converted into pollen and condensed by the bees into honeycomb, Violet heard part of the explanations and stories told by the

Fairy Queen. Actually, she was hardly paying attention and had very little memory of the diabolical plan devised by the Oppressive Forces of Music.

It was a perverse, long-term investment which, if it had had one hundred percent success, would have guaranteed the victory of darkness. The strategy had been very intelligent and had operated with the most powerful weapon of darkness. The weapon of despair. What the Oppressive Forces of Music wanted was to make people believe that it was no longer worth making an effort or fighting for a better world.

The musical forces in the Castle must have noticed that in the Kingdom of the Blue Earth and in many other kingdoms everything was being dominated: human beings were only interested in sensations, and the stronger and coarser the better. Thus they would always be ruled by the law of taking advantage of everything, by vulgar or tacky music or even by the classics that had been born sick from depression or hate.

Yes, the Oppressive Forces knew they had to deter all styles and inclinations. However, the simpler and more palatable the structures of music consumed were, the easier and cheaper it would be to dominate the masses.

This Mass domination was crucial and, therefore, it was more than opportune to control all means of dissemination. They needed to corrupt who they could and in any way they could.

The subjects of the Queen of Western Music were not corruptible by money, fame or power. However, if the virus of despair contaminated them, the Oppressive Forces would achieve success. That was how, astutely and subtly, they had been blowing the lethal virus in the wind and dust for hundreds of years.

At first, not even the Fairy Queen noticed their tricks. A few were contaminated. But, little by little, the sickness was growing even under the watchful eyes of the Guardians of the Towers. Subtly, the virus spread inside the Castle. A virulent pandemic broke out. Despondency was the first symptom. Despair followed and soon total apathy, which made the population become zombies, asleep against their will. This was the reason there was no-one – apart from the Guardians, who were immune to any sickness of the spirit – to defend the Castle.

The work of keeping order and inspiration in things and good music had fallen onto the queen's shoulders. She looked in vain in magic and science for an antivirus to such devastating despair. On one of these searches she learned that in the Marsh of Wild and Primitive Myths there could be a seed of faith, the size of a mustard seed, and the recommencement of evolution. If she studied and mastered the magic science of this seed, perhaps she would be able to solve the problem. She had gone countless times to the Marshes, looking for the basis of an antidote. Obviously the spies working for the Fairy Queen of Totalitarian Music informed their mistress, receiving gifts of sensations in return. The constant comings and goings of the Fairy Queen helped the Oppressive Forces to hatch another plan: capture the Fairy Queen. That would be far from easy. However, if very well planned and executed at a moment of carelessness or sadness, it could work. This is what had happened decades before Violet's journey to the Kingdom of the Seven Moons.

That is to say that the Fairy Queen had been struggling for almost eighty years to get free. Her imprisonment had been a great advantage during the second half of the 20th century in the Kingdom of the Blue Earth and in other Kingdoms that were not evolved. The Fairy Queen of Music was very powerful and, even though taken by surprise, she had not stopped fighting for herself and for a world free of totalitarianisms, said to be well intentioned or not. She fought as much as she could, but for sure she had lost ground: a desert was gnawing at the limits of the Green Valley, and her direct subjects were becoming apathetic.

That was when she was inspired as to a possible cure for her subjects. She had summoned a fragile, disinterested and pure child from the Kingdom of the Blue Earth to re-ignite the flame of hope. Her strong magic allowed her to communicate with one of her bravest female soldiers in the Castle, who had refused to succumb to the illness of despair. She told her where the three magic tuning forks were. She ordered her to find a special child, who could be the bearer of a new flame.

Joaquina wandered for thirty years, from score to score, from school to school, from conservatory to conservatory, throughout the Kingdom of the Blue Earth, always summoning a child. However, she had never found the ideal soldier. When a boy or girl had succeeded in the first stages, the Fairy Queen of Easy Fame had devoured them with false promises. Thus, they had never managed to free the Fairy Queen.

The quaver continued for decades, until one day, disheartened, she heard a father and daughter playing at composing a story about impossible love between a man and woman from countries that were at war with each other, a stupid war like all the rest. They called that music *Opera*. It was the first opera that Violet would compose. That so-called opera was something simple and primary, and should never have been called opera. However, there was a certain ingenuity and a dream at that moment which moved the quaver, as determined and courageous as any woman, mother and breadwinner. Here was her last hope.

It must also be said that all the previously chosen children, when they failed or were even devoured, returned alive to the Kingdom of Earth. Everything they experienced in the Kingdom of the Seven Moons was nothing more than a terrible nightmare for them.

But Violet's journey was different. The realm of the Fairy Queen of Music emptied along with her strength and, consequently, the dimensional barriers that separate the Kingdoms were becoming more rarefied. The parallel and distinct realities of the two dimensions were getting closer. From that moment, if the life of a traveller in the Kingdom of the Seven Moons was in any danger, the dangers would be the same in the Kingdom of the Blue Earth. It was possible to understand the lacerating pain, worse than a branding iron, which Violet's mother had felt in her womb moments before, when her daughter had died, only to come back to life afterwards.

We should say that, even before deciding, Joaquina returned many times to that apartment to follow the emotion and unfolding of that so-called opera, performed by a fledgling pianist and an amateur saxophonist. She was enchanted, not by the music, but by the spirit of the music. This was how the eight-year-old girl with the German Piano was chosen. And this was how the same girl inspired everyone.

It was Violet's valour and hope for a cure, the great magic, that freed the army and the Fairy Queen herself.

But, as we've already said, the reasons given by the Fairy Queen were of no interest to Violet. In fact, she didn't pay much attention to the reasons. Much less to the to the explanation about the agreement that the Fairy Queen of Easy Fame had made with her cousin the Fairy Queen of Real Fame. Both had agreed that they would not interfere with the girl's journey after she reached the top of the mountain, as long as Violet passed the fame test. Naturally, the Fairy Queen of Easy Fame would never keep to her part of the bargain, despite having had so many victories in diverse kingdoms that it couldn't possibly be a mere curly-haired girl who would thwart her plans and put her in the Tyrant Fairy Queen's bad books.

Violet was happy and didn't want to know any of this or any other reasons still not explained in this story. Without forgetting the longed-for beans, she was bursting with boundless energy thanks to the honeycomb given to her by the Fairy Queen.

CHAPTER XVI

BACK TO THE CASTLE

What can a child facing such great evil power do other than inspire hope? And isn't hope the only cure for that worst of ills, despair?

"Mission accomplished ∞ ♪ ♫ ♥ ! Mission accomplished, my faithful Joaquina and my valiant Pedrão ∞ ♪ ♫ ♥ ! Let us finish the other mission not yet over ∞ ♪ ♫ ♥ !

"That's it. Let's get them. Let's go."

"No, you won't be going this time, my best and most valiant winged soldier ∞ ♪ ♫ ♥ !

'Why not?"

"My dear warrior, they would never have succeeded without you∞ ♪ ♫ ♥ ! The war has been cruel for the flowers∞ ♪ ♫ ♥ ! And butterflies are pollinators∞ ♪ ♫ ♥ ! We need your work for the time being ∞ ♪ ♫ ♥ !

"But I'll work double afterwards. Allow me, my Queen, to protect them with my life."

"Please let him go with us. Let him, dear fairy, let him go. Please!"

"Yes. He's a great warrior!!!!!!!!!!!!!!!! He's a show-off, but he's a good warrior!!!!!!!!!!!!!!!!!"

"Please. Let him!"

Violet was looking up into the Fairy Queen's face. She was smiling with the typical look of a child who's requesting something. Joaquina tried to imitate Violet's expression and all she managed was an irrepressible shamefaced, nervous smile. Pedrão rested on the girl's shoulders and stayed there with his restored wings half open, puffing out his chest to impress.

The Fairy Queen gave in, but her look imposed silence, with no celebrating. Afterwards, she raised her arms and closed her eyes. She began to sing. The singing was accompanied by a piano. The sound had emerged from nothing and the wind then blew. It blew from the east. It didn't take long for enormous eagles to be seen. They came from the far west, beyond the Desert of Dead or Forgotten Music.

They were eagles made of flower petals. Their bodies comprised all types of petals possible. They could alter the density and rigidity of the petals at will. Sometimes they had the gentleness of flowers, other times they became rigid as if the petals were stones.

Their beaks were made of the strongest keratin known. Their claws were made of unbreakable spines from giant cacti, able to tear through even the metal of a war ship. Their eyes were two sunflowers the size of balls used for elephant football. Eyes that allowed them to see beyond the line of the horizon and even a little beyond the line of time.

And talking about time, it was a very long time ago that in the Kingdom of the Seven Moons they were known as the eagles of the Valkyries. This is because they were often seen being ridden by warrior muses, inspirers of justice and heroic feats.

The legends and myths surrounding the Valkyries travelled through and were adapted in the most diverse worlds. On planet Earth, in Nordic mythology, the Valkyries were the servants and messengers of the Lord of the gods Wotan, or Odin. Pre-Christian Germanic peoples, as the Vikings did, defined them as beautiful young immortal beings who rode their winged horses, armed with helmets and spears, flying over battle fields. They would gather the bravest warriors who had fallen in battle and take them to the palace of Valhalla, governed by Odin, to help in the final war of all times. The Vikings also believed that the aurora borealis was caused by sparks from their armour and helmets while they were riding in the sky.

Nordic mythology was what inspired one of greatest musical geniuses – maestro, composer, theatre director, essayist – the German Wilhelm Richard Wagner to compose the libretto and music for the majestic work 'The Ring of the Niberlung' (*Der Ring des Nibelungen)* between 1848 and 1874.

The cycle of 'The Ring of the Nibelung' is a tetralogy comprising four operas in chronological order: The Rhinegold, Valkyrie, Siegfried and Twilight of the Gods.

In appearance, the Valkyries of the Kingdom of the Seven Moons had much in common with the warrior goddesses of mythology. They were also muses that inspired heroic feats and acts of justice. They only became involved in a conflict when the balance of justice tipped too much in favour of the powers of darkness. Even so, they made their presence known when they were not on a mission throughout the diverse Kingdoms.

They, who also loved Wagner's work, at a certain moment in the past, no one knows why, stopped riding their eagles in order to mount winged unicorns. However, the Eagles of the Valkyries always were and will be their beloved allies.

So, in decisive moments of war or dangerous missions, the Eagles continued to be summoned. And, if summoned, they never faltered. We should say that it was an eagle chick that brought the Fairy Queen's message to Violet and Joaquina, when they left the Marsh of Love. But at that moment it was the adult eagles that came to bring the message that the Valkyries had also woken from despair. Soon they would arrive for war,

Violet and Joaquina were goggle-eyed at the aerial formation. It adorned the blue heavens and helped to dissipate the pain that lingered insistently like dense mist in the Marsh.

None of this magnificence made Pedrão feel as content as when he saw what was following the eagles. They were giant butterflies made of flowers, comprising four huge Victoria-amazonicas connected in life and will by the stems and bodies of grouped bromeliads. Their heads were composed of a thousand flower petals, where two eyes made from sunflowers, with wonderful vision, were shining.

The magic of the flower eagles and butterflies was incredible. Dispersed, they were just flowers. Together, whether in the form of butterflies or eagles, they had lives and souls unified in just one being. Both the eagles and the butterflies wished to defeat the Oppressive Forces, which used the power of the plant world for illicit purposes such as the production of drugs.

Violet noticed Pedrão's smile of pride and satisfaction. He was puffing out his chest more than ever. She understood the reason for this pride and spoke in a low voice just for Pedrão to hear:

"You're think you're really something now, don't you?"

Without losing his pose and speaking even more quietly, he replied:

"It's the power of the butterflies. You'd better believe it. It's our turn now!"

"Oh, my goodness. You must be joking. I love you, little butterfly. No, I mean to say, I love you Pedrão."

"At your command, my queen". It was the voice of the eagle leader, which had landed in front of all of them and folded its wings, creating a puff of air scented with wild flowers. Following the eagle leader, the biggest butterfly repeated the gesture and words. The remainder of the two air forces began to fly in circles, creating moving shadows on the soil of the Marsh.

"Well done, old friends. ∞ ♪ ♫ ♥ ! Thank you for answering my call. ∞ ♪ ♫ ♥ ! Violet, Joaquina and Pedrão, come with me ∞ ♪ ♫ ♥ !"

"Majesty! Majesty! I'm sorry to bother you, but I believe I should fight in my division. Don't you agree? May I fly with my comrades?"

"He wants to be part of the butterfly squadron!!!!!!!!!," Joaquina whispered in Violet's right ear.

The Fairy Queen of Music almost never got angry at her subjects' requests. She knew how to understand the mind and desires of beings, whether plants, animals, men or angels. It is certain that she did not grant a request when she did not agree with it, but she always had a way of saying no and making them understand without offending this or that one's pride.

"Very well∞ ♪ ♫ ♥ ! But flying in formation with them could cost you your wings again ∞ ♪ ♫ ♥ ! I promise that one day you'll be as big as they are because your courage and character already are∞ ♪ ♫ ♥ ! But let's do this ♪ ♫ ♥ ! You and the butterfly leader go together and promise me that you'll stick to his neck like glue no matter what happens ∞ ♪ ♫ ♥ !

After witnessing Violet coming back to life, this was the happiest moment in Pedrão's short life. With all the respect of a soldier for a general, he saluted and flew to the neck of the giant butterfly, saying:

"My captain, my commander, in life and death I am at your side. This is my greatest honour!"

It was such a solemn utterance that it impressed everyone. With the power of a plane and the lightness of a hummingbird, the butterfly flapped its Victoria-amazonica wings and set off in flight…

"Stay with me, warrior, and don't let go" Pedrão heard from the butterfly leader.

The Fairy Queen took Violet's and Joaquina's hands, moving close to the eagle. First Violet, then Joaquina and last of all the Fairy, to take care of the other two, sat on the eagle's back. She gave the command:

"We have a Castle and then a Kingdom to save∞ ♪ ♫ ♥ ! May God help us∞ ♪ ♫ ♥ !"

If the butterfly got to the skies quickly, don't even mention the eagle. Not even the smartest hummingbird could accelerate so much and not even the swiftest peregrine falcon in its mortal dive could fly as that eagle did. Violet's abundant hair covered Joaquina's eyes through the force of the wind, and the note complained not at all because she was breathless: there was so much emotion and fear. Holding onto the eagle's thick neck, Violet noticed something unique. It was as fluffy as a pillow of flowers. Being so soft, it flamed a desire to stroke the eagle. But when she put a little more pressure on, the flowers became as hard and sharp as diamonds.

"Wow, that's incredible" the girl said, observing and feeling the eagle's plumage. But as soon as they got to twelve thousand metres, the scenario caught her attention. The Fairy magic was protecting the human and the quaver from the effects of the cold and the low pressure. They were flying quickly over marshes and mountains.

A little ahead lay the snowy hills at mid-altitude that formed the natural division between the Green Valley and the Nameless Marsh. The Castle was many kilometres beyond these. It seemed far away, but time and distance shortened with the swift wings of the eagles and butterflies. They passed over snow-capped hills. It was the loveliest view that Violet had ever seen: ice, valleys and rivers of rocks, home to trout, beavers, marmots, squirrels, falcons and wolves. Soon they were approaching the air space over the battle field.

The battle was raging all around the Castle with other colours and sounds. As the inhabitants woke up, the battlements gained defenders. If on the one hand, the Oppressive Forces performed their nefarious music with their instruments, now trumpets and horns made up the heavy artillery on the side of the defenders. Violins, violas, and double basses also executed the counter attack.

The Green Valley witnessed the full war of sounds, notes, music. Strident guitars on one side, guitar solos on the other. Drums against drums. It was rock'n roll against rock'n roll, blues against blues, while notes and more notes clashed and fought in the air. The war had now become more even and no one could say for sure who would be victorious in the end.

But when the Oppressive Fairy Queen had arrived minutes beforehand, flying with her stinking gases and her very powerful negative energy, the frightened armies made more effort. Fear of her was so great that those under her command preferred death to seeing her face in its Medusa version. She went behind the attacking forces and began to conduct an orchestra of two thousand brainwashed musicians with enslaved souls. In that macabre orchestra, the men wore jackets and the women wore long black dresses. They might have looked elegant, but anyone who drew near could see that their clothes had never been washed. The orchestra played louder than all the rest.

In the centre, standing on the conductor's rostrum, was the Fairy Queen of Totalitarian or Oppressive Music, holding three batons and conducting her war machine. The rest of the army and the artillery, coerced and motivated by tyranny, advanced under the heavy fire coming from the top of the walls. The pianolas began to laugh again. The catapult operators accelerated the bombardment of the same bubbles used in the Garden of Flowers. The invading army now intended to climb over the Castle walls, forming a mountain of rubbish in front of them. All who had died or had become lame were thrown there for this purpose.

That was when the eagle and butterfly air force arrived. The first eagle to arrive was carrying the Fairy Queen, Joaquina and Violet. After a quick aerial reconnaissance, it landed on the Tower of G Major. The Fairy Queen handed over Violet and Joaquina to the care of the Guardian of the Tower without a word. They understood one another without needing to speak.

Seconds later, Violet and Joaquina, standing at the Tower window, almost a thousand metres up, could see the eagle in the skies and the battle unfolding and taking lives in the Valley at the foot of the Tower

Then, the butterflies arrived and began a bombardment of fruit with melodic seeds. This fruit, when in sufficient number, annulled the effects of the pitch bubbles, making them enter into a rapid process of biodegradation. This was very painful to the ears of the baboons, men and women, forcing them to writhe on the ground.

The effect was devastating to at least ten thousand enemies. The chief pianola protected itself, using some women who were operating catapults at its side as a shield.

Three hundred instrument operators began anti-aircraft fire. They had no effect on the butterflies, because these were quick and flying very high. They almost always managed to swerve and it would take more than an occasional bullet from a mutilated note or deceitful music to scare them. To the despair of the chief pianola, the bombardment continued, as did the casualties.

"Damned dragons, where are you? Aren't you going to do anything you "*merlecas*," you ugly slime balls?.

"*Merleca*" was one of the swear words normally used by the pianola when addressing those under its command. The dragons already knew their target. They were afraid of the butterflies, but even more so of the pianola. Only their dread of the Oppressive Fairy Queen was greater than the fear whipped up by the pianola. So they fired themselves with determination and went up higher. Their baboons were preparing the artillery that now had to be well-aimed.

The butterflies didn't falter. They kept on flying in the direction of the sky above the Tyrant Fairy's orchestra.

Pedrão, holding onto the butterfly leader's neck as tight as he could, yelled:

"Come on, you foul-breathed creatures. I still have enough sleeping pollen for all of you."

The butterflies didn't swerve a millimetre from their routes. This meant they would soon be hit by the baboon artillery and by the dragon teeth, right in the belly or neck because these were gaining altitude. The fearless butterflies now diminished their speed to increase the precision of their new bombardment, which would be dropped onto the macabre orchestra. The dragons' teeth were getting closer and many shots from mutilated notes were already hitting their wings. It was two hundred dragons against a hundred butterflies.

"Srambamm! Strambamm! Strambamm............."

One hundred tremendous, hissing sounds of short duration were heard. The only way to write them is more or less this:

"Strambamm! Strambamm!"

They were caused by one hundred eagles, which, diving from an altitude of fifteen thousand metres, like fighter jets protecting bomber planes, dug their claws into the dragons' necks. Taken by surprise, the dragons had their heads torn off, to then fall in a spiral with their baboons, crashing into their own army.

The remaining one hundred dragons, which had come flying one hundred and twenty metres below the aerial line of attack, were not intimidated and proceeded to wage war against the butterflies.

Everything happened very fast after that. As soon as each one of the dragons went to sink their wild boar's teeth into the necks of the butterflies, the latter partially bent their front wings backwards, creating an enormous aerodynamic brake. This made the dragons miss their targets and pass by, grazing the butterfly necks, which were now inclined backwards.

In less than a hundredth of a second each butterfly whipped or beat their wings in the dragons' ears. As they say in fight slang each one gave such a good smack in the ear, that those which didn't pass out were disoriented. That was the time necessary for the eagle squadron to return and repeat even more easily with the last hundred dragons what it had done seconds before with the first hundred.

"Ahhhhhhhhhhhh! Now I want to see you chasing children and attacking flowers!" Pedrão celebrated, and in his enthusiasm one of his feet came away from the butterfly leader's neck, and unable to withstand the pressure of the wind, he spun backwards. Luck and sheer will power helped him to get to the Tower where Violet and Joaquina were. He was welcomed like a combatant in dire straits. Dumbstruck, the three proceeded to watch everything from their private box.

The butterflies hit the coordinates of the target and scattered an even greater quantity of fruit with melodic seeds over the orchestra. But this time it was without any effect at all.

The orchestra music had already begun and its enchantments and dark magic too. A strong dark energy was creating a field of impenetrable music. It was creating an evil bubble. Now no seed dropped by the butterflies achieved its objective. They were all toasted. The eagles and butterflies did their best to penetrate, but the dark energy was burning. Because of this, they had to give up the attack on the orchestra and fight on the battlefield near the wall.

Since the butterflies had no ammunition left, they joined the eagles in the hand-to-hand fighting. One of them, getting too close to the ground, suddenly had fierce, rapid hemidemisemiquavers swarming all over its back, wanting to perforate its Victoria-amazonica wings.

The butterfly reared up, howling in pain and shook its wings violently. Just three of the notes fell off. The others continued with their perforating incisions of noxious vibration. That was when one of the eagles collided on purpose with the butterfly's back and grabbed four notes from above.

Without losing flight speed, it gained height and did a loop manoeuvre. At the very moment that it was upside down with its extended claws holding the notes, squirming continuously, another eagle flew by in the opposite direction. The claws made from giant cactus of both eagles touched for instants, ripping apart forever the poor enslaved musical notes.

Two other butterflies came with their powerful wings to whip the notes, which were still clinging to their comrade's back.

Seconds later the butterfly was free and flew off to recoup and return to combat.

Flying on the eagle's back, the Fairy Queen of Music noticed a new danger. The action of the Oppressive Fairy had become suicidal. She was intoning atomic war music, whose radioactive waste lasts for more than five thousand years. She wanted to poison everything and everyone. Her success would leave the Castle uninhabited, the two armies destroyed. And what would she gain from that? Nothing, apart from revenge and its bitter taste that sours the mouth of anyone who takes it.

The Fairy Queen of Music decided to use her conducting talents. The immense eagle hovered in the air and she began to conduct the wind. Meanwhile, the evil bubble of energy was growing and at first touched the Oppressive Fairy's army. The pianolas and smarter generals, as well as some knowledgeable baboons, took refuge at the feet of the orchestra, inside the source of the bubble and away from its evil effects. Effects so evil that the unfortunates who were hit trembled and became full of energy. Thus, they became virtually invincible. However, you could be sure that minutes later they would be writhing on the ground in a slow death.

So as not to have the same end, the eagles and butterflies gained altitude and only just escaped from the bubble. As the invading army became entangled in it, the screams became more horrendous. With a frenetic and irreversible death wish, they threw themselves into suicidal attacks. Their instincts told them that it was preferable to die then from the artillery fired from the Castle walls than wait for the painful effects of contamination.

Therefore, when hit by the bubble, they speeded up their marching and began to run to be cut to pieces or do the same to their enemies.

The Fairy Queen of Music continued her conducting. Sounds of another gigantic orchestra rose to a crescendo. They were produced by all the wind instruments we know and those that we will know one day. The fifes and tubas tuned up and played low and high sounds in counterpoint. The violins and cornets came in. Where did they come from? From the very magic nature of the Kingdom of the Seven Moons would be the most precise answer. It seemed that they came from the very blowing of the air between the clouds, or from the trees in the forest where Violet had passed.

"The Ride of the Valkyries," the most famous excerpt from the Opera "The Valkyrie," by Wagner, was beginning. And this made the hair of any living being that had fur or hair stand on end. The words sung by the Fairy Queen were not the same as those in the opera on Earth. She was speaking of things we cannot understand.

At that moment, another leader appeared from the distant clouds, in an aerial gallop. She was mounted on a spectacular white horse, which arrived snorting, with its single horn as hard as steel. The leader turned her neck to look at what was behind. A formation of white and black horses, all winged and ridden by her sisters, was following her. They were the Valkyries, who appeared at the same time that the music conducted by the Fairy Queen became stronger and more audible.

They were all coming in a synchronized aerial galloping movement. They were holding lyres the size of harps and were dressed in the mythical clothes of goddesses of war, including silver helmets in the form of small wings. Shin protectors and breastplates made from an alloy of platinum and titanium, flexible but unbreakable, made up part of their apparel. On their backs they carried shields forged in solar furnaces. Veils and skirts covered their elongated bodies from the waist down. Large, fearless, tall, and eagle-eyed, they radiated Nordic beauty.

A large volume of air entered and seconds later was expelled through the nostrils of the muscular winged stallions, whose black eyes registered the desires of their warrior souls, unaccepting of chaos. Their manes shook in the wind, as did the fire and gold coloured hair of the combatants.

From the Fairy Queen's point of view, the squadron was getting close fast. But for Violet, Joaquina, Pedrão and the Guardian at the window of the Tower of G Major, the details described here weren't so clear. However, they did have a panoramic view of the scene. Astonished, they observed that the Valkyries were soon hovering, divided in equal numbers beside the Fairy Queen. They heard the music increasing dramatically in volume, while cumulous clouds took on the form of musical instruments.

The song of the Valkyries joined the playing of the orchestra conducted by the Fairy Queen.

An ecstatic Violet remembered the concerts she had attended in the Kingdom of the Blue Earth and concluded that this spectacle was incomparable. She turned to the other window in the Tower. Her hair blew in the wind. Even though she was at an altitude of almost twenty thousand metres, she was able to observe the world below with precision.

Through some unknown mystery, her eyes had partially acquired the vision of the eagles. There were many defending the Castle on the wall parapets. They were men, women, dwarves, nymphs, mythical beings and musical notes – each one was holding some kind of instrument and was firing against the oppressive army.

"They'll see. Their intentions are very bad. Joaquina, are we going to win? There are more of them than us, aren't there? But will we win?"

"Yes we will" said Pedrão in her ear.

Joaquina came towards her. She was smiling so as to hide her concern. She didn't succeed. Violet was perceptive and Joaquina was a bad actress.

Then Violet ran into her arms and hugged her. Pedrão almost fell off her shoulder.

"Yes we will! We will! My daddy always told me that faith is everything. He always spoke about hope. About never giving up. We *will* win."

She was speaking for herself and everyone else. The Guardian of the Tower looked tenderly at the girl. A noble-looking, serious giant who a few seconds before had sparked the curiosity of the girl, was now intrigued at the strength of the little human's hope.

Violet, Joaquina and Pedrão noticed that the other Castle Towers had also become the source of sound and magic. With the arrival of the Valkyries, the other Guardians lost no time and hammered their tuning forks. Accompanying the music being performed, some produced a reddish light and metal sounds, as if they were immense percussion cymbals. Others, accompanying the symphony, radiated a sky blue light and resonated like drums from a samba school in Brazil. The Guardian of the Tower of G Major did the same with his giant tuning fork. There was a tremor and cracks in the ground of the Green Valley swallowed up many of the attackers contaminated by the evil bubble.

That was when a new light appearing from the epicentre of space, where the Fairy Queen and the Valkyries were hovering, began to radiate. At first it was a very strong golden radiation that hung over the dark, sick radioactive bubble, which was growing ever larger and was approaching the wall. From the centre of this radiation, a ball of light, also golden and dense, was forming. Inside it, many rays in tones of yellow, violet and pink ricocheted as if in a chain reaction of light. By the way, an unbridled reaction of light would be a more appropriate description for that photonic, magical phenomenon.

Just as the radioactive, sticky pitch bubble was growing like an out-of-control atomic reactor, the other was expanding in a chain of light.

They soon met, and mortal subatomic battles of principles and will began combat. Illness against health. Hope versus despair. Love against hate. Music against music. Both were equivalent in strength and neither gave up ground.

"Smother them, Vranduorf! By the magic and music of all the dark souls," sentenced the Tyrant Queen, who had awoken Vranduorf, calling for her favourite dragon. Her secret weapon up to then, well guarded and fed with all the malice, hate, lies, sickness, depression, envy, sadism, flesh and blood of the slaves acquired for hundreds of years. Vranduorf was the degenerate result of many different breed crossings, in which the main DNA had been badness combined with selfish male and female chromosomes. He had come into the Oppressive Fairy's hands still very little, as a gift from one of the Tyrants of the Underworlds. She had given him to her son as a pet at first. Decades later, when he had already grown alarmingly and she noticed the danger that Magmamute himself was in, she decided to build a large cave after the desert adjoining the Green Valley, and kept him there in secret. Her intention was to use him at the right time. And this time had arrived. Her magic command travelled to the distant lands of the north, where she was already reigning in the Kingdom of the Seven Moons.

The size of an Olympic athletics track, Vranduorf the dragon emerged from the Cave of the Abyss. His face resembled that of other dragons because of his pig-like muzzle. But his teeth and jaws were more like a hyena's. His head was the size of four elephants put together. He had the body of a lizard, four legs with feet like a white gecko's and the wings of a vampire bat. But the most bizarre part of his body was known only to a few of the Tyrant Fairy's subjects. Between the joints where his wings met his trunk, a flap of tough, spongy skin like a turkey's wattle, had formed. It was connected to the oesophagus, where internal organs similar to our glottis regulated the flow of air. If stretched, the flap measured about fifteen metres. When this improbable being so wished, these flaps inflated when his wings were spread and acquired a curious outline: they looked like two saw-edged cornets stuck to the dragon's body.

A deafening boom. Frightening screams. Vranduorf took flight. A shadow like an eclipse on the desert floor moved quickly in the direction of the Green Valley, which we should now call the Valley of Torment.

Accompanying the sinister dragon, came four hundred more dragons in combat formation, intoxicated by the effects of *coorraína*. When Vranduorf entered Green Valley airspace, he repeatedly contracted his wings against his own thorax. A sound shock wave was fired against the Fairy Queen and the Valkyries. The closest sound we know would be the twisting of metal after a collision between two armoured warships. Accompanying the wave, a rapid jet of dust contaminated by billions of tiny mites, which fed on the mortal remains of skin and souls, spilled over all of them. In the Kingdom of the Seven Moons the physical, magical and spiritual worlds were strongly interconnected. These mites contaminated any soul that was not very, very determined against the virus of depression.

The Fairy and the Valkyries protected themselves, directing part of their strength against the sound shock wave followed by contaminated dust. The distance between them and Vranduorf, five kilometres, was decreasing. As were their attacks against the killer bubble generated by the Tyrant Fairy.

The eagles and butterflies counter-attacked and encountered the dragons in far greater numbers. The sky was a confusion of clashes.

That was when the Valkyrie leader and six of her sisters uttered their occult enchantments. They left the aerial formation that was producing the golden bubble of golden light. This then weakened. They rode towards the North, towards Vranduorf. The route was for a head-on collision. Their harp-sized lyres turned into long, flaming swords. Each one a specific colour and note, all on fire. They forged ahead with their arms gripping their platinum and titanium shields.

None of the dragons molested them or got close to them, because they had ten eagles in formation as an escort. The dragons wouldn't have the courage.

Vranduorf directed the fire of his negativity precisely. The Fairy Queen of Western Music took her focus away from the dark bubble and radiated her magic onto the Valkyries. They resembled a comet of fire of all tonalities. Their horses turned fiery red and spat blazing blue flames from their nostrils. Valkyries and horses were the head of the comet. The magic of the Fairy Queen formed the crown and the tail of the comet, which resonated the music of the Ride of the Valkyries. It was as if Wagner himself were conducting the orchestra of his dreams in his theatre without limits.

One kilometre, five-hundred metres, a hundred metres. They were miniscule in size compared to the dragon. Fifty metres. The eagles dispersed. The dragon snorted, his teeth slimy with stale blood. There was no time for him to react. A comet made up of Valkyries in flames hit him. Passing through the dragon, they exploded his heart.

Protected by the magic of the Fairy Queen and by the energy of their swords and shields, the Valkyries suffered nothing, other than a sudden and violent acceleration, due to the contrast of vibration of semi- spiritual materials that differentiated their bodies from the body of the dragon. They were hurled violently more than five hundred kilometres away.

Two howls, one of anger, the other of pain, could be heard. That of the Tyrant Fairy and that of the dying dragon, splattered on the ground. This provoked a mini-earthquake. After this event of seismic proportions, a tornado formed in the body of the dragon, which quickly absorbed his matter and evil. As soon as it did this, the tornado headed towards the black bubble in order to deposit all the evil energy there.

The Fairy Queen and the remaining Valkyries saw the growth in the negative strength of the dark bubble. As for the Tyrant Fairy, she went crazy. She was laughing and behaving like the most theatrical conductor, moving and conducting emphatically. Occasionally, strands of her Medusa hair grabbed some of her musicians and brought them to her mouth to be devoured.

Her orchestra instruments were boiling hot, due to the huge amount of energy demanded of them. The poor lips of the trumpeters. The scorching mouthpieces burned their lips, which would soon be sealed because of all the blisters. But fear and the ingested *coorraína* kept them playing incessantly, like lunatics.

For the Tyrant Fairy nothing else mattered. She was laughing out loud. After all, her evil music was winning. The bubble of golden light, weakened by the absence of the Valkyries, no longer restrained her. There were just a few metres left to reach the castle walls and infect everyone there in one go.

The dark bubble was approaching. Violet and Joaquina hugged each other. Joaquina tried to cover the girl's eyes so that she wouldn't see her own end and that of everyone and everything. Violet wouldn't let her. Afraid, Pedrão stayed quiet on the girl's shoulder. In each other's arms, Violet and Joaquina cringed together, waiting for the end. The sound was deafening and the queen's cackling and the screams of the desperate echoed around the castle.

Once again Violet thought of home. Perhaps because she was facing death, the memory of her mother and father was more alive than ever. More and more happy moments from her life passed before her eyes. She could remember in broken flashes the time when she was still in her mother's womb and her father would rest the saxophone against her mother's belly and play really low. Soon after came the affective memory of mother's milk and the scents of her two grandfathers. She had lived so little time with them because even before she was two, they had left for other planes. She thought her grandmothers were so sweet and adorable. Each one was so different from the other. One chubby and active, always wanting Violet to eat a bit more, always saying she was too thin. And the other, so calm but at the same time worried about her. How she loved her grandmothers. She knew that, if they could, they would give their lives for her. She also remembered the lady who had worked in her house and what a great friend she had been. Her godfather, godmother, cousins, school pals, her best friend in the building. The ice-cream at the corner and the games of tig with her father. She always felt furious and at the same time challenged because he never let her win. He would run and run and was often more of a child than she was.

The life of any human really is so rich in small, but immense everyday, affective treasures, yet we human beings, still crawling in evolutionary terms, almost never value them as we should. It's common for us to give too much value to what we don't have and forget to love and be grateful for the infinity of blessings we receive daily.

For a few instances, at this crucial moment, Violet began to see all the events in slow motion. She even had time to let a tear of farewell fall for her loved ones. She prayed for them and asked Our Heavenly Father to bless everyone.

A vision of a very faraway place appeared before her eyes. At first, she thought she'd seen her beloved piano. But she soon realized it was her mother and father sleeping. They were having restless dreams. Each one in their own way was having nightmares that always resulted in separation from their daughter. She felt such pity and nostalgia and once again asked our Heavenly Father to watch out for them. The vision vanished into mists of an uncertain future and soon time returned to normal speed and to the present.

The dreadful end came near, materialized in the dark bubble. Joaquina held Violet tighter. In his last gesture of valour, Pedrão decided to puff out his chest and spray the bubble with the sleep-inducing pollen. A cold, foul-smelling wind invaded the Tower.

The Guardians, with their muscular arms, and sweating heavily, hammered their tuning forks with the maximum physical force in their bodies and souls. Castle defenders aimed their artillery at the bubble that would devour them. They shot at close range but nothing made any difference. The notes were promptly burned and absorbed as soon as they collided with it. There was so much rubbish piled up in front of the wall that it helped the invading soldiers to climb up. There was more hand-to-hand fighting between notes, men, women and baboons on top of the wall.

All seemed lost, but the missing seven Valkyries returned at speed from where they had been propelled. In no time at all they were in formation again. In the sky, the Fairy Queen and the Valkyries sang even louder. The golden light intensified its powers. At each sustained, high-pitched note sung by one of the Valkyries, or at each plucking of the strings of the magic lyres, a strong fork of lightning or electrical discharge of one million volts was projected from the skies towards the bubble.

Flashes blocked out the Sun itself. The Seven Moons were then seen in the full light of day. Everything fed the defending light. The reverberating sound of the orchestra had reached its peak for any ear, human or not. The Tyrant Fairy continued with her macabre cackling.

From the lips and throat of the Fairy Queen a trill capable of cracking all the crystal in the world perforated the dark bubble, heading towards her rival, who had to take refuge behind a gigantic pianola covered in musicians like half-alive, half-dead shields.

The Fairy trill, the lightning caused by the Valkyrie lyres, the sounds of the tuning forks from the Towers and the great melody fused together in the bubble generated by the enslaved orchestra. A whirlwind of luminous shocks of energy of life and death clashed and the radioactive bubble shrank, imploding on itself like a black hole. Seconds before the end, realizing imminent defeat, the conductor grabbed the piano leader with one of her tentacles and simply said:

"To hell with everything!!! I'll be back. I always come back!"

Followed by the dragons that had survived the confrontation with the eagles and butterflies, she flew off to places unknown in the Kingdom of the Seven Moons. Her orchestra and army had been destroyed and the valley floor cleaned of dirt. Now it would just be a question of time for the Green Valley to go back to being the Greenest Green Valley in the universe.

, A giant roar of celebration could be heard coming from the castle. Blessed by the Fairy Queen, the Valkyries, eagles and butterflies flew to their homes, happy at one more mission accomplished. Peace had now returned to the Kingdom of the Seven Moons.

CHAPTER XVII

THE PARTY

When everything was over, soon after the departure of the Valkyries and their companions, a silence was heard, so deep that you could even hear the beating hearts of Violet and Pedrão. They were beating very fast. After two long minutes the people in the Castle celebrated the victory noisily, while a strong wind swept away the dust of war.

Violet was taken to a very special guest room. As soon as she arrived, she found herself standing before a huge bed. And as she was exhausted, she fell asleep the moment her head hit the pillow. A whole night of darkness, a whole day of light. When she awoke and opened her eyes, she noticed that the bed had sheets perfumed with lavender and wild flowers. The pillows were fluffy. The afternoon light came in through two wide windows.

"Bath time!!!!!!!!!!!!!!"

Joaquina said this without getting up from the armchair where she was sitting.

"Hello Joaquina. How are you? What do you mean "bath time?""

"Time to have a bath and get ready!!!!!!!!!!!!!!! We're having a party today!!!!!!!!!!!!!!!"

"If we're having a party, how come you don't look happy?"

Violet got no reply whatsoever from Joaquina. She went to the bathroom, where a jacuzzi full of warm rose-perfumed water, with the addition of mineral salts of health and hope, awaited her.

She lay there for more than half an hour and finally getting out, she noticed something incredible. Her wounds, scratches and bruises had healed without her noticing a thing. Joaquina brought her two fluffy white towels and a new pair magic slippers. Her clothes were already clean and as new as if they'd just been sewn and embroidered. Minutes later, with her hair still wet and dripping down the back of her dress, she heard:

"Aren't you going to comb it?????????"

"No".

"Why not???????? You have to comb it!!!!!!!!!!!!!!!!!"

"I don't want to. It's better like this!"

"But you have to get the tangles out at least!!!!!!!!!!!! It'll look like a bird's nest!!!!!!!!!!!!!!!!!!"

"You sound like my Granny. I like my curls."

"But you can't go like that!!!!!!!!!!!!!!! How can a girl not want to get the tangles out of her hair??????????

"There's too much chattering and not enough action. It's seven o'clock and the party's already started without us. I didn't face frozen air and dragons to be looking at all this. Since when was this so important?"

It was Pedrão's voice that rang out when he flew into the room and landed on the towel rail.

"Hi Pedrão? How are you?"

Then Violet allowed Joaquina to pass the comb through her hair five times at the most from crown to ends until on the last stroke one of the teeth got stuck in a large knot of entangled strands.

"Ouch! That's enough. Enough. I can't stand anymore. You're hurting me."

"Mmmmmm. Stubborn girl!!!!!!!!!!!!!!!!!!!!! It's going to get worse!!!!!!!!!!!!!!!!!!!!!!!!"

"No it won't. I like my curls."

"Women!"

Pedrão had the last word. The two came out of the bathroom and went through the bedroom door. They were followed by Pedrão, flying right behind them. They got to a very long, wide corridor, with alternating windows and balconies. They were in one of the side buildings, which housed two-hundred guest bedrooms.

'It's this way, my little friend!!!!!!!!!!!!!!!"

Joaquina showed the way to one of the balconies. When Violet arrived, she could see other internal buildings. She saw streets, squares and gardens.

"How lovely! But what now? What do we do? Joaquina, why are you so quiet? Are you sad?"

The quaver gave a short unconvincing smile and said:

"Look, they're coming !!!!!!!!!!!!!!!!!!!!!!"

A carriage formed by four immense arum lilies joined together by a gigantic sunflower came flying towards the balcony. The structure of the carriage was unique: each flower was connected by a petal from a sunflower, four metres in diameter.

Joaquina and Violet, with Pedrão on her shoulder, climbed to the balcony parapet and jumped into the magic flower carriage. They sat in the eye of the sunflower. The yellow pollen released stayed shining on Violet's dress for a long time.

A firefly the size of a child served as the driver and sat on the edge of one of the lilies at the front. Pedrão landed on the lily on the left and there he stayed. Without a word, the firefly gave the carriage a command and the vehicle accelerated so fast that Violet saw nothing of the route: she was more concerned with holding on. She just noticed that they were flying over squares, parks and streets. Some of the streets reminded her of those in small mediaeval cities. Others were wide, tree-lined avenues with a multitude of inhabitants coming and going. Inside the walls of the Castle of Western Music there were houses and buildings of the most diverse styles. However, each neighbourhood or sub-district maintained a unique architectural style so as to preserve the visual and sound harmony of each part of the fortress.

The carriage stopped in front of the steps of the Castle's main building, called the Palace of Polyphonic Harmony. Fifty musical notes formed two rows in profile along both edges of a flight of one hundred steps. These steps linked a square full of flowers to an immense gothic arched door, which marked the entrance to the palace. Proudly holding peace lilies, the notes seemed to be holding swords, like soldiers on Earth when they wish to honour someone.

The trio went up the stairs, impressed by the reception and the frames of golden dragons and lions adorning and guarding the heavy wooden doors.

They passed through two enormous anterooms, where paintings with images of rivers, mountains and orchestras – which seemed to be alive and emitting sounds – decorated walls more than twenty metres high. When they reached the main banquet hall, the sound of French horns, trumpets and tubas solemnly announced them, followed by a chorus of more than a thousand voices.

"Viva! Ten vivas and ten hurrahs for the Girl with the German Piano, who saved everyone."

Violet received a standing ovation, while wind instruments accompanied the great hurrah.

"Long live the note Joaquina for her dedication and endless strength of will!"

A new collective ovation shook the solid palace columns. When they thought there would be silence:

"Ten vivas and ten hurrahs for the most heroic butterfly in all the kingdoms!

Flushed and happy, Violet, Joaquina and Pedrão were then fed by the energy of gratitude and admiration.

"Approach without fear my children, my heroes ∞ ♪ ♫ ♥ !"

It was the motherly voice of the Fairy Queen of Music, now seated on a throne at the extreme end of the hall opposite of the entrance. The three timidly crossed the two hundred metres of the hall, where a diversity of beings bowed to them: gigantic flowers, birds of diverse species, pollinating insects, cheetahs, fauns, elves, dwarves, wolves, men, women, musical notes and many other different creatures.

They sprang up the twenty steps that took them to the throne and knelt respectfully before the Fairy Queen. She stood up and opened her arms. The gentle, intense and melodious voice flooded the hall:

"Let it be known to all on the side of right ∞ ♪ ♫ ♥ ! Let it be proclaimed throughout the Kingdoms where our music reaches ∞ ♪ ♫ ♥ ! Let it be recorded in the scores of time and beyond time so that it will never be forgotten or erased from memory ∞ ♪ ♫ ♥ ! Those who fight for good, will always be loved and remembered by the good ∞ ♪ ♫ ♥ ! Today the Seven Moons, all the stars and those here present will be witnesses to our gratitude to these three heroes ∞ ♪ ♫ ♥ !

While the Fairy Queen was speaking, subtle aromas of rose and jasmine spread through the hall. Then, close to the palace ceiling, cotton-like clouds appeared, images in the mist of the condensed aromas. They were scenes of streams, waterfalls, fields of flowers, suckling mothers, fathers running with their children, fruit budding and ripening in orchards, elephants roaming the savannahs, whales singing, fireflies and so many others appearing and disappearing in a turmoil of joy. They were images of health and freedom. Visions and more visions of life.

The Fairy Queen then directed her gaze to a small girl, a musical note and a butterfly. The images on the ceiling vanished. A violet and gold light flowed from the palms of her hands and fell upon the three happy honoured guests:

"I name you, Violet, Dame of the Sacred Order of Pianos. And I name you Joaquina, Grand Dame of the Music that Protects Children∞ ♪ ♫ ♥ ! And you, my warrior butterfly, I name you Grand Master Knight Lord of the Kingdom of Butterfly Guardians of the Life of Flowers ♪ ♫ ♥ ! Arise, Violet, Joaquina and Pedrão, for now we are the ones who honour you ∞ ♪ ♫ ♥ !"

The hall was filled with collective acclamation, accompanied by the sound of instruments, which lasted more than seven minutes. Applause and such exclamations as "Bravo!" were also heard many times. The girl from the Kingdom of the Blue Earth radiated joy and Joaquina managed not a word. As for Pedrão, this was the only time that butterfly cried in his whole life.

"Let the party begin ∞ ♪ ♫ ♥ !"

Music flooded the atmosphere while arum lilies flew over the space, serving anyone wanting to feed on their magic liquid.

A choir of adopted orphan children, singing lilies and violets, blackbirds and thrushes intoned melodies that would be played one day in the Kingdom of the Blue Earth. The fusion of children's, plant and bird voices was moving. The finely tuned warbling of throats sang of the health and the sublime beauties of the universe. Much later, it was learned that even the angels, who never stop working for the good of the worlds, and who were passing by invisibly at the time, stopped to appreciate the music.

Touched by the timbres of the voices of hope, Violet wanted to compose or play something. Filled with emotion, she allowed some tears to fall, which, together with the tears of emotion shed by others present, began to float and gain height in the immense hall. It was as if it were raining from the floor upwards. However, it was rain in slow motion made of drops of water that sprang from eyes. Each tear shone in a different colour, according to the emotion of its owner. Though produced by the tear glands of the listeners, the real founts were their souls.

Replete with paintings and ornaments, the palace ceiling exhibited works painted by Michelangelo, Leonardo da Vinci and sculptures by Antonio Francisco Lisboa, better known by his nickname, Aleijadinho[6]. These were just some of the many artists of the sublime who helped to compose that unimaginable scenario

When the rain of tears reached the palace ceiling, small rivulets of coloured lights formed. They ran across the ceiling and joined together until a great river absorbed all the rivulets. This river advanced along the ceiling

---

[6] Little cripple: From Minas Gerais, he was a sculptor, carver and architect of the colonial Brazilian Baroque style. He is considered the greatest sculptor in the Americas from the Baroque period.

towards the main entrance and there fell in a splendid ten-metre waterfall. This cascade did not touch the steps of the palace stairway. Less than a metre from the ground it halted its fall. Curving, going against the law of gravity, it flowed towards infinity, carrying prayers, requests, health and hope to the most distant Kingdoms, places or souls in need.

The choir proceeded with three more songs and was applauded at the end. Then there was a short silence. The curtains opened and the stage of a grand theatre came into view, as did the orchestra. Musicians and instruments, stools and the conductor's rostrum were supported by Victoria-amazonicas of all sizes, hovering at different heights. The orchestra comprised two hundred string, wind and percussion instrumentalists. At the first level, seven grand pianos were positioned in front of the conductress.

Seated on their respective piano stools, seven very old gentlemen were waiting. They were dressed in the classic style of erudite musicians. It wouldn't be possible to say exactly how old they were. But it was immediately noticeable that they were men with noble souls and a great intensity of happiness. Their expressions denoted this.

However, the conductress, also dressed in gala clothes, appeared younger. She signalled with her baton and began conducting. At first, only the pianists played. And how they played. Their souls, their bodies and the souls of the pianos became one. They were more than virtuosos. Our ears will still have to evolve considerably to appreciate that concert. The multiple melodies performed blended together so harmoniously that they joined in the air as drops of water unite to form an ocean.

The speed and intensity were so great that some strings actually burst into flames because of the high temperature. The only reason the pianos didn't catch fire was because they were made of magic wood and metals. After ten minutes, the rest of the orchestra sprang into action, with intoxicating performances.

That was when, at the conductress's command, there was a silence that would deafen any listener. Two great side doors opened and a sound like the "ra-ta-tah, ra-ta-tah, ra-ta-tah" of the soles of shoes stamping against the palace floor invaded the air. The rhythm and intensity of the beginning of the tap dancing increased slowly.

When Violet realized what it was, she rubbed her eyes to see if it really was true: a ballet corps, composed of women and human-sized carnations – whose stems forked, forming two legs – entered the hall with synchronized movements and the sound of tap dancing in unison. Accompanying the dancers, fifteen female violinists beside the carnations and fifteen men with soprano saxophones were walking side by side.

A great "Yee-haw!"was heard when the saxophonists and violinists began a joyful musical duet in Celtic Irish style. The music performed was an accolade to Earth and the life force of all mothers on Earth. Human and flower dancers gave a show that was a feast for the eyes.

The dancers tap danced as free, proud and light as wild deer in the Irish woodlands or the Scottish mountains. The carnations, though they were flowers, were virile and leapt like hunting tigers. When the women and carnations embraced and twirled, the world seem to spin with them. The saxophonists and violinists formed pairs in an endless duel. No one, anywhere in the universe, could have been happier than they were at that moment.

A half an hour later, the orchestra resumed playing with all the instruments and the festival of music and dance became collective. The river of tears of emotion was then inundated by an even bigger wave of love transpired by everyone. Just one light was present, in which colours alternated their nuances. First, the Palace was lit up. Then it was the entire Castle and after that from the Kingdom of the Seven Moons a new irradiation, as strong as a supernova, spread through all dimensions and kingdoms.

CHAPTER XVIII

THE GRAND PIANO IN THE BANDSTAND

The party was in full swing and the first rays of sunlight were running down the slopes of the distant hills. That was when Violet noticed for the first time in a while that she didn't have Pedrão on her shoulder or flying close by.

The Fairy Queen read her mind and drew close to her:

"Go to that balcony, my dear∞ ♪ ♫ ♥ !"

Violet walked twenty paces until she saw, on the balcony parapet, a lovely monarch butterfly speaking to more than a hundred thousand attentive butterflies. They were perched in trees, on roofs and everywhere they could rest.

Pedrão was talking like an army general about to set out on his mission, which in this case was to help reconstruct the lives of the flowers destroyed in the war.

The girl was impressed with Pedrão's hauteur. Even so, she interrupted him, as she usually did:

"Hi, my friend, I don't want to bother you. But I just wanted to know where you were."

Pedrão turned round. The one hundred thousand butterflies didn't move their wings a millimetre, but they all looked at Violet.

Violet understood that moment and what would come next. It was her first goodbye. A goodbye with the fragrance of raspberries and roses. She didn't know if this goodbye was a happy or sad one, but she felt it was profound.

"Were you going to leave without saying goodbye?" she said, pouting.

'Of course not!"

"But why did you come out here alone?"

"To prepare the squadron".

The one hundred thousand butterflies continued to look at the girl and their new commander. Pedrão continued:

"If I weren't a butterfly but a human, I'd wait for you to grow up to be your boyfriend and marry you."

"But you're my little pal, aren't you?"

"Not so much of the little, no. I'm big and strong. I'm a Queen's Knight."

"OK, OK. So to be a big pal you don't need to be a person, it's enough to be a big pal."

She bent her face and kissed Pedrão's head. His wings trembled and he smiled. The squadron of one hundred thousand butterflies did the same with their wings.

"Goodbye dear friend, I love you very much

"Bye-bye my friend. Bye-bye my brave Knight Lord of the Kingdom of the Guardian Butterflies of the Life of Flowers. Did I get that right?"

The butterflies had begun to flock and Pedrão had to leave to command them and guide them in the great reconstruction. Violet saw them rise in flight, just as the first rays of sun brought the day. The cloud of monarch butterflies blocked out the dawn, but gave that morning an unequalled light. Pedrão looped the loop and landed for seconds, for the last time, on the girl's shoulder and she gained one single kiss on the cheek. It was a kiss from the butterfly, who then beat his wings and flew away. In a few seconds he was up high and leading the squadron. Where destiny and evolution would take him, and if he would meet Violet again one day, only all-knowing God was privy to.

Violet made to enter the hall again but Joaquina, followed by the Fairy Queen, went to the balcony. The Fairy Queen stayed silent and Joaquina was serious.

"So it's goodbye for us as well?" said Violet, choking and sobbing sadly. She ran to hug the Fairy, who lifted her into her arms. She felt a maternal tenderness and missed her own mother.

The Fairy Queen put her back down on the floor and remained in silence. It was not necessary for her to speak for Violet to recognise her love and eternal gratitude. Joaquina also stayed quiet and serious. Violet ran to hug her friend. Again, the threat of tears stifled her child's voice:

"So you mean it's all goodbye? Just goodbye now?"

"Goodbye for real and forever, no!!!!!!!!!!!!!!!!!!!"

"What do you mean? You always half say things, when you should say everything."

"Goodbye for real is for those who don't know if they'll see each other again!!!!!!!!!!!!!!!!!"

"But what do you mean?"

"If you really want to and you study a lot, you'll be an incredible pianist and composer!!!!!!!!!!!!!!! And this will unite us forever!!!!!!!!!!!!"

"But will I see you again?"

"Like this, seemingly not!!!!!!!!!!!!!! The Fairy Queen hasn't given me any assurances!!!!!!!!!!!!!!!!!!!!"

Violet creased up her face to cry. And that's what she did. But in a restrained way. Tears flowed, but she soon controlled herself until her expression became even sadder and the crying came back stronger than before.

"Let's have none of this, my friend!!!!!!!!!!!!!!!!!!!! No sadness!!!!!!!!!!!!!!!!!!!! True love and friendship are never lost!!!!!!!!!!!!!!!!!!!!!!! It's forever!!!!!!!!!!!!!!!!!!!!!!!!!! And we'll always be friends!!!!!!!!!!!!!!!!!!!"

"But I won't see you again."

"Like this, no!!!!!!!!!!!!!!! But the other way, yes you will!!!!!!!!!!!!!!!!!!!

"What do you mean, like this no but yes I *will* see you?"

'Whenever you're playing or studying and a note seems to shine and move on your score, you'll know it'll be me encouraging you to go on."

Violet gazed towards infinity with her nose running. She looked like a poor abandoned girl. Once again she hugged her friend and finally smiled at the Fairy Queen.

"I'm ready. I know, something magic is going to happen, isn't it?"

The Fairy Queen and Joaquina smiled tenderly at this display of human smartness. The carriage appeared. Joaquina jumped inside and Violet did the same. The journey to one of the Castle's squares was short, and there was a bandstand in the centre. Violet didn't understand how, but as soon as she got out of the carriage, the Fairy Queen was there. A band was playing in her honour and an accomplished pianist with a wonderful grand piano was part of the band.

At that moment the sounds of the piano enveloped them. Joaquina extended her hand and Violet took it. Everything turned blue, pink and red and a tumult of pentagrams from an unknown score embraced Joaquina and Violet. The Kingdom of the Seven Moons disappeared from their view while another space and another time appeared.

In a flat in the city of São Paulo, a piano was playing by itself. Violet saw herself very small beside Joaquina inside the piano, surrounded by luminous rays. The strings were being hammered and were playing an unknown melody. A carpet formed by visible sound waves took them outside the piano, at the very moment the piano lid opened, only to close again.

Chocolate, the dog from the neighbouring flat, was the only witness to hear the magic phenomenon. She barked and scratched the door without stopping. A derivation of light and sound passed under the two doors that separated the dog from that room and touched her muzzle, ready to smell everything except luminous music. She stopped barking at once, ran under the sofa and stayed there.

In the next flat, Violet was taken floating to her bed. She was suddenly her normal size and dressed who knows how in her original pyjamas. Joaquina gave her a final kiss.

At that moment, a small design appeared on her pyjamas. Between elephants and bears there were two embroidered magic slippers. They cast a long-lasting spell. That was why those pyjamas took a long time to wear out.

The piano became silent as soon as Violet began her journey back. The day dawned in São Paulo and Violet ran to her parents' bed to hug them and snuggle there a little, getting warm and nestling between them. From that morning, whenever Violet was tired or unenthusiastic when studying her piano, she could swear that a quaver seemed to shine and move between the bars. This was how they communicated ever after.

♪ ♪ ♪

Made in the USA
Middletown, DE
13 November 2023

42619908R00116